Historical Account of Every Sect of the Christian Religion

SALZWASSER VERLAG

J. S. C. De Radius

Historical Account of Every Sect of the Christian Religion

Reprint of the original, first published in 1864.

1st Edition 2022 | ISBN: 978-3-75259-400-3

Verlag (Publisher): Salzwasser Verlag GmbH, Zeilweg 44, 60439 Frankfurt, Deutschland
Vertretungsberechtigt (Authorized to represent): E. Roepke, Zeilweg 44, 60439 Frankfurt, Deutschland
Druck (Print): Books on Demand GmbH, In de Tarpen 42, 22848 Norderstedt, Deutschland

RELIGIOUS SECTS.

WITH THE

LIST OF SUBSCRIBERS

ADDED AT THE END.

HISTORICAL ACCOUNT

OF

EVERY SECT

OF THE

CHRISTIAN RELIGIO

ITS

Origin, Progress, Rites and Ceremo

WITH

A BRIEF DESCRIPTION

OF

JUDAISM AND MAHOMETANI

COMPILED FROM THE LATEST AUTHORITIES.

BY J. S. C. de RADIU

SECOND EDITION (REVISED).

1864.

TO THE READER.

The Christian world is divided into denominations, each of which is discriminated by sentiments peculiar to itself.

To delineate the nature, point out the foundation, and appreciate the tendency of every individual opinion would be an endless task. The design of the publication is, therefore to enumerate briefly the leading tenets of the parties which attract our notice.

It is presumed that the outline will greatly interest the general reader, as well as those who will read solely for instruction, especially as throughout the work no opinion is expressed regarding the merits or demerits of any peculiar faith, the intent being to present the reader with an impartial narrative of facts, selected from the best authorities, and which forming part of history, may quicken inquiries after truth.

To reflect upon the origin, progress, persecutions, and final *triumph* of True Religion, over the darkness of *ignorance*, of the cruelties engendered by superstition.

cannot fail to excite in the mind of every thinking Christian, an increased feeling of veneration for his faith, and of gratitude to the Supreme Disposer of events, who has been pleased to terminate the long night of error, and to purify the minds of men, whose hands are no longer raised to persecute for religious differences their fellow men, but are grasped in amity, to dispense the blessings of His "Holy Word," to the uttermost ends of the earth.

INDEX

TO

THE CHRISTIAN SECTS.

JUDAISM AND MAHOMETANISM.

THE

CHRISTIAN RELIGIOUS SECTS.

ABYSSINIAN CHRISTIANS.

ORIGIN.—The general conversion of the Abyssinians to Christianity is supposed to have taken place about the middle of the fourth century, when Athanasius was Patriarch of Alexandria.

PROGRESS.—In the seventh century they embraced the sentiments of the Monosophytes, and were looked upon as a pure church.

In the fifth century, the Portuguese having opened a passage into the country of the Abyssinians, this was selected as a favourable opportunity to extend the influence of the Roman Pontiff. The same important commission was also given to several Jesuits, but both missions failed, the Abyssinians remaining firm to the faith of their ancestors.

About the commencement of the seventeenth *century*, the Portuguese Jesuits renewed the mission to Abyssinia, but their cause was ruined by the intemperate zeal of one of the Abyssinians, whom they had created a Patriarch. Since that period, every attempt made by the Romanists to regain a footing in Abyssinia has proved unsuccessful.

The Christian population, of which the priests are supposed to form the twentieth part, is said to amount to 3,000,000; and but few members of this church are to be found in other countries.

TENETS.—The Abyssinian Church receives the holy Scriptures as the perfect and the only rule of faith and practice. They worship one God in Trinity; they believe in the incarnation of the Son of God; that Christ is perfect God and perfect man; and that his merits are sufficient for eternal salvation. They admit that the Holy Spirit, though a distinct person, equally existed from eternity with the Son as with the Father; but they maintain that He proceeded from the Father only.

RITES AND CEREMONIES.—Their festivals and saints are numberless. As they celebrate the *Epiphany* with peculiar festivity, in commemoration of Christ's Baptism, and sport in ponds and rivers, some have supposed they undergo baptism every year. One of their saints' days is consecrated to Balaam's ass; another to Pilate and his wife, because Pilate washed his hands before he pronounced sentence on Christ, and his wife desired him to "have nothing to do with the blood of that just person." They have four seasons of Lent; the great Lent commences ten days earlier than ours, and is observed with so much severity that many abstain even from fish, because St. Paul says, "There is one kind of flesh of men, and another of fishes."

Prayer for the dead is common, and invocation of saints and angels; and such is their veneration for the Virgin, that they charged the Jesuits with deficiency in this respect.

On going to church, persons put off their shoes before they enter the outer precinct. Devotees kiss the threshold or the two door-posts on entering; they then enter, and say what prayer they please, and their individual duty is over.

Excommunication, in Abyssinia, expressly *prohibits* the person on whom it is pronounced from kindling a fire, and every one else is restricted from supplying him with fire or water. No one can speak, eat, or drink with him, enter his house, or suffer him to enter his own. He can neither buy, sell, nor recover debts; and, if he were slain by robbers, no inquiry would be made into the cause of his death, nor would his body be allowed to be buried.

ANTINOMIANS.

ORIGIN.—The founder of this sect was John Agricola, a Saxon divine: having obtained a professorship at Wittemburg, he first taught Antinomianism there, about the year 1535, his doctrine being, that the law is nowise necessary under the gospel; that good works do not promote our salvation, nor ill ones hinder it; that repentance is not to be preached from the decalogue, but only from the gospel.

They derive their name from *anti*, against, and *nomos*, law, as being against the moral law; *not merely as a* covenant of life, but also as a *rule of conduct* to believers.

PROGRESS.—This sect sprang up among the Presbyterians in England during the protectorate of Oliver Cromwell, who was an Antinomian. About the same time it obtained many converts among the Churchmen in America, where it prevails considerably at the present day.

During the last century, its doctrine was embraced by some of Mr. Whitfield's preachers, and others, and subsequently by William Huntingdon, who was acknowledged as the head of the sect, and the celebrated Dr. Hawker, of Plymouth, who, it is believed, was the first of his school who avowed himself an Antinomian and gloried in the name. To the influence of his preaching and writings may be ascribed the spread of these opinions in the West of England, chiefly within the pale of the Established Church, which led, in 1818, to the secession of several clergymen from the establishment, who formed themselves into a distinct body of "Separatists."

The Antinomians are supposed to be an increasing sect, both in England and Wales.

TENETS.—The following are the principal

doctrines which bear the appellation of Antinomian:—

I. That justification by faith is no more than a manifestation to us of what was done before we had a being.

II. That men ought not to doubt of their faith, or question whether they believe in Christ.

III. That by God's laying our iniquities upon Christ, and our being imputed righteous through him, he became as completely sinful as we, and we as completely righteous as Christ.

IV. That believers need not fear either their own sins or the sins of others, since neither can do them any injury.

V. That the new covenant is not made properly with us, but with Christ for us; and that this covenant is all of it a promise, having no conditions for us to perform; for faith, repentance, and obedience are not conditions on our part, but on Christ's; and that he repented, believed, and obeyed for us.

VI. That sanctification is not a proper evi*dence* of justification; that our righteousness *is nothing* but the imputation of the righteous*ness of Christ.*

ARMENIANS.

ORIGIN.—The Armenian Church dates its foundation from the fourth century, when, according to the native annals, Tiridates the Great, with a large portion of his subjects, received baptism from St. Gregory, surnamed Loosavorich, or "The Enlightener."

PROGRESS.—In the beginning of the sixth century, the Armenian Church seceded from the Greek Church, of which they formed a branch, and became independent. From that period Armenia has undergone many revolutions, that have affected their religion more or less.

The Armenian Church was shaken to its foundations in the seventeenth century by the barbarous policy of Shah Abbas, King of Persia, who forcibly transplanted thousands of Armenian families to different parts of Persia, laying waste all that part of Armenia that was contiguous to his dominions, in order to place an unpeopled wilderness between his realms and those of his Ottoman rivals. In the general emigration that ensued, the more opulent Armenians removed to

Ispahan, where the Persian monarch granted them a residence, with the free exercise of their religion, and where they have a considerable monastery (the seat of a bishop) at this day. The successors of this monarch were not equally generous. Persecution ensued, and many of them apostatised to the Mohammedan religion. On the other hand, their numbers greatly increased in different parts of Europe, where a vast proportion of Armenians had fixed their residences for the purposes of commerce, and who were not unmindful of their brethren in the East. From Amsterdam, Marseilles, and Venice, they were supplied with Armenian translations of the Holy Scriptures, and other theological books. These being judiciously dispersed among the Armenians who lived under the Persian and Turkish governments, contributed to preserve the numerical strength of the sect.

Besides the religious societies of the Armenians in their own country, and in Turkey, where they are very numerous, they are to be found in every principal city in Asia. They are the *general merchants of* the East, and are in a state of constant motion from Canton to Constantinople. They are settled in all the principal places of India, where they arrived many centuries before the English. The commerce of Persia is chiefly conducted by Armenians. They are also very numerous in Russia, at St. Petersburgh, Moscow, and Astrachan, and are to be found in the Caucasian Governments. They have, besides, small societies in London and Amsterdam.

Wherever they colonise they build churches, and are exemplary in their conduct and religious observances.

According to the latest and most exact returns, the Armenian nation numbers about 1,900,000 souls, who, previously to recent territorial changes, were thus distributed:—In the Russian provinces, 52,000; in Turkey, 1,600,000; in Persia, 90,000; in India, 70,000; in the Austrian dominions, and other parts of Europe, 26,000.

Tenets.—The doctrine of the Armenians differs from the orthodox Christians chiefly in *their* admitting only one nature in Christ, and believing the Holy Spirit to issue from the Father alone.

The doctrine of the Armenian creed, respecting the person of Christ, is, that "God, the Word, became perfect man, one person, and one united nature; God became man without change, and without variation."

Rites and Ceremonies.—The rites and ceremonies of the Armenian church greatly resemble those of the Greeks. They mingle the whole course of the year with fasting; and there is not a single day which is not appointed either for a fast or a festival. They commemorate our Lord's nativity on the 6th of January, and thus celebrate in one festival his birth, epiphany, and baptism.

The Armenians practise the trine immersion, which they consider as essential to baptism. After baptism, they apply the *enyrop* or *chrism*, and anoint the forehead, eyes, ears, breast, palms of the hands, and soles of the feet with consecrated oil, in the form of a cross. Then they administer to the child the eucharist, with which *they only rub* its lips. The eucharist is celebrated only on Sundays and festivals. They do not mix the wine with water, nor put leaven in their bread as the Greeks do. They steep the bread in the wine, and thus the communicant receives both kinds together.

They worship after the Eastern manner, by prostrating their bodies, and kissing the ground three times. When they first enter the church, they uncover their heads, and cross themselves three times; but afterwards they cover their heads, and sit cross-legged on carpets. The greatest part of the public divine service is performed in the morning, before it is light. They are very devout on vigils or feasts, and on Saturday evenings, when they all go to church; and, after their return home, perfume their houses with incense, and adorn their little pictures with lamps. They invoke their saints with prayers; reverence and adorn their pictures and images, and burn to them lamps and candles.

PAPAL ARMENIANS.

ORIGIN.—We find that so early as the *fourteenth* century a Roman Catholic Archbishop was sent to Armenia to govern the church, by Pope John XXIII. The present Armenian Catholic Church was founded in this manner, and is, in fact, a branch of the Church of Rome. Of this communion, the Armenian Catholic Patriarch, who resides at Constantinople, is the head under the Pope.

PROGRESS.—After this singular event some Armenian ecclesiastics succeeded in raising a persecution, which terminated in the banishment of the Jesuits. The ambassador's influence, however, restored them to the field of their labours, and early in the last century they had extended their operations so widely, that the mission was divided into two branches.

The Papal Armenians now form a very considerable body, although they are not now numerous to the east of Tokat and Trebisond. At Teflis, in Georgia, is a convent of Capuchin missionaries, with a congregation amounting to 1,000. At Angora they formerly amounted to many thousands. At Smyrna, between 3,000 and 4,000 are said to be of the Romish communion; and at Constantinople and the adjacent villages the Roman Catholics now average about 7,000.

ARMINIANS.

Origin.—This sect arose in Holland by a separation from the Calvinists, and derive their name from James Arminius, an eminent professor of divinity in Leyden, about the year 1600.

Thinking the doctrine of Calvin with regard to Free-will, Predestination, and Grace, inconsistent with Scripture, Arminius began to express his doubts concerning them in 1591; and upon farther inquiry adopted sentiments more nearly resembling those of the Lutherans than the Calvinists.

Progress.—The controversy thus begun, became more general after the death of Arminius in 1609, and threatened to involve the United Provinces in civil discord. The Arminian tenets, however, gained ground under the mild and favourable treatment of the magistrates of Holland, and were adopted by several persons of merit and distinction. In 1610 the Arminians presented their *Remonstrance* to the States of

Holland and West Friezland, specifying their grievances and praying for relief; and in 1614 the States issued an ordinance directing the Remonstrants to live in love and charity with each other. But as both parties doubted the obligation of such a decree in respect to spiritual affairs, the famous Synod of Dort was held from November, 1618, to May, 1619, in order to adjust the differences. By this synod, in which politics got mixed up with religion, the Arminians were considered as enemies to their country and its established religion, and were exposed to much persecution. They were treated with great severity, and deprived of their posts and employments, their ministers were silenced, and their congregations suppressed.

After the death of Maurice, Prince of Orange, in 1625, the Arminian exiles were restored to their former reputation and tranquillity; and under the toleration of the States, which was granted them in 1630, they erected churches, and founded a college at Amsterdam, which *produced many* able divines and sound scholars. *The Arminians* were subsequently exposed to occasional persecutions, during which their sect was very numerous, but when they had gained liberty and peace it began to decrease.

Arminian tenets were known and adopted in Great Britain at a very early period. Archbishop Laud is well known to have greatly encouraged them; and after the ejectment of nearly two thousand ministers, for not complying with the Act of Uniformity, the Church was almost wholly Arminian. By far the greater part of the clergy of the Establishment have taken this side of the question; and the term Arminian is applied by many as descriptive of the doctrines of the Church of England.

The members of the Episcopal Churches in Scotland and America, the Moravians, the General Baptists, the Wesleyan Methodists, the Quakers, and the Swedenborgians, are Arminians.

In France, Geneva, and many parts of Switzerland, they are still numerous.

TENETS.—The distinguishing tenets of the Arminians are comprised in the five following articles, relating to Predestination, Universal

Redemption, the Corruption of Human Nature, and Perseverance.

I. That God from all eternity determined to bestow salvation on those who, as He foresaw, would persevere unto the end in their faith in Christ Jesus; and to inflict everlasting punishments on those who should continue in their unbelief, and resist to the end of life his divine assistance.

II. That Jesus Christ, by his sufferings and death, made an atonement for the sins of mankind in general, and of every individual in particular; that, however, none but those who believe in Him can be partakers of that Divine benefit.

III. That true faith cannot proceed from the exercise of our natural faculties and powers, nor from the force and operation of free-will; since man, in consequence of his natural corruption, is incapable either of thinking or doing any good thing; and that, therefore, it is necessary, to his conversion and salvation, that he be *regenerated* and renewed by the operation of the *Holy Ghost.*

IV. That this Divine Grace, or energy of the Holy Ghost, begins, advances, and perfects everything that can be called *good* in man; and that, consequently, all good works are to be attributed to God alone;—that, nevertheless, this grace, which is offered to all, does not force men to act against their inclinations, but may be resisted, and rendered ineffectual by the perverse will of the impenitent sinner.

V. That God gives to the truly faithful, who are regenerated by His grace, the means of preserving themselves in this state;—that the regenerate may lose true justifying faith, fall from a state of grace, and die in their sins.

BAPTISTS.

ORIGIN.—The true origin of this sect, according to Mosheim, is hid in the remotest depths of antiquity, and is extremely difficult to be ascertained.

Some of the Petrobrussians in the twelfth century, some of the Lollards, or Wickliffites, in the fourteenth, and some of the Hussites in *the fifteenth*, were Baptists in sentiment. But, these few instances excepted, the existence of *Anti-Pædobaptism* seems scarcely to have taken place in the church of Christ till a little after the beginning of the Reformation, when a sect arose, whom historians commonly called the *Anabaptists*.

PROGRESS.—In 1522 the Anabaptists of Germany began to attract attention; their leaders and themsevles, however, are considered by the Baptists of the present day as a political or revolutionary cabal. Their opinions they propagated and maintained with enthusiastic zeal and boldness, and at length even by force of arms, until their ringleader was put to an ignominious death in 1536. These fanatics also created great disturbances in Sweden.

There were at the same time Anabaptists of a very different character, who were confounded with these deluded people, and who, owing solely to their peculiar views of baptism, were at that tumultuous period the victims of revenge and persecution.

The modern descendants of those harmless and *pious men,* who then suffered with the guilty, are the Mennonites in Holland and the Anabaptists in France. Their sect greatly increased in both Holland and Germany, through the exertions of Menno Simon, from whom the Mennonites derive their name, who laboured among them with such unwearied zeal and success, until the period of his death in 1561, that he has been styled on the Continent "The Parent and Apostle of the Baptists."

The Anabaptists met with much opposition in Switzerland from the two reformers, Zuingle and Calvin, as well as from others.

The first mention of the Baptists in English history is, as the subjects of persecution, in the reign of Henry VIII. In 1535, fourteen Hollanders, refugees, were accused of being Anabaptists, and were put to death; ten others escaped the same fate only by recantation. During the reign of Edward VI. a commission was issued to try "All Anabaptists," &c. &c.; and they were empowered, in the event of their contumacy, to commit them to the flames.

Under Elizabeth the same inhuman policy was *persisted* in. In 1575, a congregation of Dutch

Anabaptists was discovered at Aldgate; many were imprisoned, and four of them made their recantation, bearing faggots at St. Paul's Cross. Eight Dutch women were shortly after banished, and two for their obstinacy were sentenced to be burned. At length, exiled by the proclamation of Elizabeth, the remnant of the Anabaptists fled to the United Provinces, where they mingled with the other Protestant exiles.

In the reign of James I. many Anabaptists fled to Holland to avoid the persecution, which was kept alive till 1611, when Legat and Whiteman were burned at the stake. The latter, a Baptist of Burton-upon-Trent, was the last martyr that suffered this cruel kind of death in England. Having been exposed to such great severities, the Baptists were slow in establishing themselves in England. In 1640 their first congregation was formed. Under the Long Parliament the Baptists did not wholly escape persecution.

On the accession of King William and Queen *Mary the Toleration* Act placed the Baptists, in *common with* other Protestant dissenters, under the protection of the laws. The Baptists have long subsisted under two separate and distinct societies, distinguished by different names; those who have followed the doctrines of Calvin being called *Particular Baptists*, and those who profess the Arminian tenets being denominated *General Baptists*.

In 1689, a general assembly of the Calvinistic Baptists was convoked in London, consisting of the representatives of one hundred congregations, who decided on putting forth a confession of faith, containing all the leading peculiarities of their doctrinal tenets and discipline, which document still remains the most complete representation of their sentiments.

In Ireland the Baptists only average about twelve churches or congregations, all of which are inconsiderable.

The Dutch Baptists (the Mennonites) are very considerable at the present day. In Holland they consist of about one hundred and fifty-six congregations, numbering 95,000. In the Prussian dominions they have a number of scattered congregations, enumerating about 16,000.

In Russia they have four churches, amounting to about 6,000. In the United States of America the descendants of Mennonite emigrants form a distinct communion, and can number more than two hundred churches, some containing three hundred members. In some parts of Pennsylvania the Mennonites compose the bulk of the population.

Baptists were found among the earliest British settlers in America, but owing to persecution they formed no church until 1639. During the first hundred years they laboured under many restrictions and disabilities, and their numbers were very small; but after the establishment of American Independence their numbers and prosperity increased rapidly. In 1812 they had, in the United States, 2,000 churches; 1832, upwards of five thousand; in 1840, seven thousand seven hundred and sixty-six. About three millions of souls, or about a sixth of the whole population, were in connexion with the Regular Baptists. In 1847 they had *established* missions in every quarter of the globe, besides a home mission, a Bible translation society, several colleges, and other religious institutions. In 1856 the number of congregations was 9,395.

TENETS.—This denomination of Christians are followers of Calvin, and are distinguished from others by their opinions, either respecting the mode and subject of baptism, or by their denying the validity of infant baptism, considering it as a human invention not countenanced by the scripture.

Instead of administering the ordinance by sprinkling or pouring water, they maintain that it ought to be administered only by immersion. Such, they insist, is the meaning of *baptizo*, to wash or dip, so that a command to *baptize* is a command to *immerse:* thus they say it was understood by those holy persons who first administered it; and thus they affirm it was administered in the Primitive Church.

The Baptists also say that baptism ought not to be administered to children or infants at all, nor to grown-up persons in general, but to those only who profess repentance for past sin and faith in Christ.

Rites and Ceremonies.—The Baptists used to administer baptism in public waters, but they now use baptisteries (as being more convenient), which are in or near their places of worship, either with the attendance of the candidate's friends only, or in the presence of the congregation; suitable dresses and separate apartments being provided for the accommodation and convenience of candidates.

GENERAL BAPTISTS.

Origin.—The General or Arminian Baptists made their first appearance in the latter end of the sixteenth century. Mr. Smith, who is usually styled "the Father of the General Baptists," became the founder of the first regularly organised Baptist Church about the year 1608.

Progress.—This class of Baptists having increased, published in 1611 a confession of their faith, diverging greatly from Calvinism.

They increased greatly at the time of the *Restoration, for* they presented a petition to

Charles II. "owned and approved" by upwards of 20,000. Soon afterwards divisions on points of belief arose among themselves, which greatly diminished their numbers, since which they have gone on decreasing.

TENETS.—On the great subject of baptism the Particular and General Baptists agree; in regard to worship and church discipline the latter differ, inasmuch as in some of their churches they have three distinct orders of ministers separately ordained; to the highest of which they give the name of messengers, to the second that of elders, and to the third that of deacons.

GENERAL BAPTIST NEW CONNECTION.

This sect has been denominated the evangelical part of the General Baptists. Their subdivision took place about fifty years ago; and according to the most recent accounts they are more numerous than their brethren, having about seventy congregations, chiefly in the midland counties, and are supposed to be on the increase.

BEREANS.

ORIGIN.—A sect of Protestant dissenters from

the Church of Scotland, who took the name of Bereans on separating themselves in 1773 from the National Church on the exclusion of their leader, Mr. Barclay, from succeeding to the benefice of Fettercairn in Kincardineshire.

They adopted the name of Bereans, from the circumstance of the believers of the gospel at Berea being highly commended for their Christian conduct in searching the scriptures.

TENETS.—The Bereans agree with the Established Churches of England and Scotland respecting the Trinity, predestination, and election; but they reject all natural religion: they take faith to be a simple credence of God's word, personal assurance they consider as of the essence of faith, and unbelief as the unpardonable sin. They consider a great part of the Old Testament as mere history, and the whole of the Psalms as typical or prophetic of Christ, and do not apply them to the experien of private Christians.

The Bereans have found but few converts to their doctrines, and form but a small and obscure *society.*

CALVINISTS.

ORIGIN. — They derive their name from John Calvin, a zealous and eminent reformer, born in Picardy in 1509, and educated at Paris. He first studied the civil law; but turning his thoughts to divinity, and finding it unsafe for him as a Protestant to remain in France, he retired to Basil, in Switzerland, in 1536, and in the same year became professor of divinity at Geneva. He soon after withdrew to Strasburg, but the Genevese earnestly inviting him to return, he accepted their invitation in 1541, when he commenced a vigorous system of ecclesiastical discipline, and continued at Geneva actively employed as a preacher and writer till his death in 1564.

PROGRESS.—Calvinism long subsisted in its complete state in Geneva, from which its tenets soon found their way into Germany, France, Prussia, and Holland, at an early period of the Reformation; and were introduced into Great Britain in the reign of Queen Elizabeth by those *divines* who fled to Switzerland to escape the *religious* persecutions of Queen Mary. But the political, and, as it has been termed, "the fanatical" conduct of that portion of the Puritans who were all rigid Calvinists, which overturned the church, brought Calvinism, already greatly on the decline, into total disrepute with the friends of monarchy in England. Since this period, however, it has maintained its ground more or less; but since the restoration of Charles II. chiefly among the dissenters.

In France Calvinism was abolished by the revocation of the edict of Nantz in 1685, but it is still professed there by almost all the reformed.

TENETS.—The essential doctrines of Calvinism have been reduced to these five, which are termed by theologians "The Five Points;" Particular Election, Particular Redemption, Moral inability in a fallen state, Irresistible Grace, and the Final Perseverance of the Saints.

Generally speaking, they comprehend

I. That God has chosen a certain number in Christ to everlasting glory before the foundation of the world, according to His immutable pur-*pose, and of* His free grace and love, without the *least foresight of* faith, good works, or any conditions performed by the creature, and that the rest of mankind he was pleased to pass by, and ordain them to dishonour and wrath for their sins, to the praise of his vindictive justice.

II. That Jesus Christ, by his death and sufferings, made an atonement only for the sins of the elect.

III. That mankind are totally depraved in consequence of the fall, and, by virtue of Adam being their natural head, the guilt of his sin was imputed, and a corrupt nature conveyed, to all his posterity, from which proceed all actual transgressions; and that by sin we are made subject to death and all miseries, temporal, spiritual, and eternal.

IV. That all whom God has predestined to life, he is pleased in his appointed time effectually to call by his Word and Spirit out of that state of sin and death, in which they are by nature, to grace and salvation by Jesus Christ.

V. That those whom God has effectually called and sanctified by his Spirit, shall never finally fall from a state of grace.

The order in which they understand the

Divine decrees has produced two distinctions of Calvinists, viz., SUBLAPSARIANS and SUPRALAPSARIANS. The former term derived from *sub*, below or after, and *lapsus*, the fall; and the latter, *supra*, above, and *lapsus*, the fall.

The Sublapsarians assert that God had only permitted the first man to fall into transgression, without absolutely determining his fall; while the Supralapsarians maintain that God had from all eternity decreed the transgression of Adam in such a manner, that our first parents could not possibly avoid that fatal event, and this as a foundation for His justice and mercy.

CHURCH OF ENGLAND.

ORIGIN.—Episcopacy was early established in England. According to Archbishop Usher, the British churches had a school or public institution in the year 182, to provide them with proper teachers. These churches kept independent of the Church of Rome until the reign of Henry I. In the 14th century arose John Wickliffe, who *has been called* "The Morning Star of the *Reformation,*" for he maintained many Protestant tenets, and wrote several tracts against Popery, besides being the first to translate the whole of the Bible into English.

But it was not until about 1530, in the reign of Henry VIII., that the Reformation is usually said to have begun in England. The establishment of the Church of England, which was the first regular Episcopal Church of the Reformation, was accomplished by slow degrees,

PROGRESS.—After the Parliament had declared Henry VIII. the only supreme head of the Church, and the convocation of the clergy had voted that the Bishop of Rome had no more jurisdiction in England, the articles of faith of the new church were declared to consist in the Scripture and the three creeds,—the Apostolic, the Nicene, and the Athanasian. The real presence, the use of images, the invocation of saints, &c., &c., were all still maintained.

During the short reign of Edward VI., the Reformation began to advance in earnest. The new liturgy was composed in English, and took the place of the old mass; the doctrines were also clearly stated in thirty-two articles. When

Mary ascended the throne all was reversed, and about 3000 of the clergy were turned out of their livings, and upwards of 500 clergy and laity perished as martyrs, while Switzerland, Germany, and the Low Countries swarmed with English exiles, who fled for their lives.

The death of Queen Mary made way for Queen Elizabeth, who replaced the Church of England on the same footing on which it was under Edward VI., and on which it now stands. As no change was made by Queen Elizabeth in the Episcopal form of government, and some rites and ceremonies were retained which many of the reformed considered as superstitious, this gave rise to many future dissensions. From the circumstance of these dissenters desiring a purer form of worship than had yet been established, they were called " Puritans," and at one time comprised many distinguished members of the English clergy.

Other sects and parties soon broke off, assuming various names, whereby the Church, during the reigns of James I. and Charles I., underwent many fluctuations. During the interregnum, in 1643, the Parliament abolished the Episcopal government, and condemned everything in the Ecclesiastical establishment that was contrary to the doctrine, worship, and discipline of the Church of Geneva. As soon as Charles II. was restored to the throne, the ancient forms of ecclesiastical government and public worship were restored. At the Revolution the established religion was acknowledged, and placed on a firm and permanent foundation; since which time nothing remarkable has occurred in her doctrine, worship, or constitution, except that in 1800, when the Churches of England and Ireland became one Church. The number of Irish Episcopalians averages 1,000,000.

From returns made in 1824, we find that the Episcopal Church in the United States amounted to 10 bishops, about 350 clergymen, and upwards of 600 congregations. The American Church has adopted the Thirty-nine Articles, without materially altering any doctrine, or the meaning of any of them, farther than local circumstances seemed to require. They reject the Athanasian *Creed*, and on points of doctrine the major part of her clergy are supposed to be Anti-Calvinists.

TENETS.—The acknowledged standards of the faith and doctrines of the Church of England are, after the Scriptures, the three creeds and the four first General Councils, the two books of Homilies, and her Thirty-nine Articles, which last are to be found in most Common Prayer Books.

Her Liturgy, or form of Common Prayer, may also be mentioned under this head, as it is doctrinal as well as devotional.

RITES AND CEREMONIES.—The Church of England allows of two sacraments only, viz., Baptism and the Eucharist.

Those called occasional offices of the Church are the Lord's Supper, Baptism, the Catechism, Confirmation, Matrimony, Visitation of the Sick, Burial of the Dead, Churching of Women, and the Commination.

The Church of England, though admitting the Eucharist as a sacrament conferring grace when worthily administered and received, does not *attach any* superstitious importance to it. This *sacrament* is generally taken by persons a little before death, as is that of extreme unction in the Roman Catholic Church; but it is administered once a month publicly in the church. The manner of its administration may be seen in all Common Prayer Books.

Baptism is the other sacrament of the Church of England, and it may be administered to either infants or adults, but generally to the former, and is either public or private. There are three services for this sacrament:—First, "The ministration of public baptism of infants, to be used in church;" second, "The ministration of baptism of children in houses;" and third, "The ministration of baptism to such as are of riper years, and are able to answer for themselves." The primitive practice for immersion is enjoined by the laws of the Church, but is never enforced. Infants receive their Christian names at this rite.

The Church of England is the established church of the British Empire, under the reign of her Most Gracious Majesty Queen Victoria. An *allusion*, therefore, of the many examples of *domestic* virtues characteristic of the reign of the present revered Sovereign, ought not to be omitted; examples so important in their influence, which appear realised.

CHURCH OF ROME.

ORIGIN.—The Roman Catholics consider the rise and progress of their Church coeval with the Christian religion. The Apostles of Jesus Christ they look upon as its founders, or rather as the Ministers employed by its Divine Founder, Jesus Christ. St. Peter they regard as the first Bishop of Rome, and the Popes as his immediate successor. The Church of Rome claims the honour of great exertions, in having early extended a knowledge of Christianity throughout the world, and ranks almost all the nations of Europe in the list of her converts.

PROGRESS.—Some of the peculiar doctrines of this church had made their appearance before the establishment of the Papal power, which is generally dated in 606, when Pope Boniface the Third assumed the title of Universal Bishop. *Some, however,* fix it in 756, when Pepin, King *of France,* invested Pope Stephen the Second with the temporal dominion of Rome and the neighbouring territories.

These were the progressive steps in the advancement of the dominion which began with the establishment of Christian religion under Constantine the Great. Rome had so long been the seat of Empire, and the mistress of the world, that it was an easy matter for its bishops to gain an ascendancy. From these humble beginnings they advanced with such well-directed ambition, that they established a spiritual dominion over the minds and consciences of men, to which all Europe submitted with implicit obedience, until their formidable power was weakened by THE REFORMATION.

The following account of the present state of the Romish Church is founded on the most recent and authentic returns.

The Roman Catholic religion is the established religion in Italy and Sicily, in Spain and Portugal, in the Sardinian dominions, in Belgium, Bavaria, and some of the minor German States, in seven of the Swiss Cantons, and in the Austrian *Empire;* in France it is predominant, as in

Ireland, and in some of the Greek islands; it is also the established religion of Mexico and the South American Republics, as of the Spanish and Portuguese colonies.

Roman Catholics are numerous in some of the Protestant States of Europe; in Russia, Turkey, and the United States; and there are Syrian, Greek, and Armenian Catholics, who acknowledge the Roman See. In India there are supposed to be upwards of 750,000, reckoning the native converts, and there are a few in China. Altogether the total number of the population within the Romish pale may be estimated at between 120 and 130 millions.

TENETS.—The Church of Rome has all along received the Apostles', the Nicene, and the Athanasian Creeds; the Creed of Pope Pius IV., containing the substance of the Decrees and Canons of the famous Council of Trent, is, however, now looked upon as the accredited and legitimate Standard of her Faith.

RITES AND CEREMONIES.—The general division of Masses is into high and low. High Mass, called also the Grand Mass, is that sung by the choristers, and celebrated with the assistance of a deacon and subdeacon. Low Mass, wherein the prayers are barely rehearsed, without any singing, and performed without much ceremony, or the assistance of a deacon and subdeacon. The music on these occasions is generally as full and as rich as possible.

The Mass used at sea is called the Dry Mass, because on those occasions the cup is omitted, lest the motion of the vessel should occasion any of the consecrated wine, which is the blood of God, to be spilled.

The Feasts and Fasts of the Roman Church are numerous, and are observed by them with great veneration and punctuality. Easter is kept with peculiar zeal and solemnity by the Roman Catholics; so is Christmas, and other holidays of that kind. Lent is also vigorously observed by them.

Every good Roman Catholic, on entering his place of worship, first dips his finger in the holy water, placed near the door; then crossing himself, gently bends the knee, looking with devotion towards the altar.

COPTS.

This name, about the etymology of which critics are of opposite opinions, has long been used to comprehend all the Christians in Egypt who belong to neither the Greek, the Armenian, nor the Roman Catholic Church in that country.

PROGRESS.—Ever since the incursion of the Saracens about the middle of the seventeenth century, when Egypt became subjected to the Mohammedan yoke, the Coptic church has been exposed to numerous severe and cruel persecutions, which have greatly diminished their numbers. The Coptic Church, however, though her members are supposed to exceed 100,000, continues, with respect to numbers and influence, the dominant Christian community in Egypt.

The Copts of the present day share with the Jews the internal trade of Egypt as general shopkeepers, brokers, agents, and farmers of the customs. They are chiefly found in Upper Egypt, where they enjoy peculiar privileges. It is remarkable that their own language, although still used in the church service, is understood by few even of their priests.

TENETS.—The Copts deny the Holy Spirit to proceed from the Son, and allow only the Three General Councils at Nice, Constantinople, and Ephesus. Respecting the person of Christ, they acknowledge but one nature and will in Him, "after the union of the Deity and Humanity."

RITES AND CEREMONIES.—They have seven sacraments: baptism, the eucharist, confirmation, ordination, faith, fasting, and prayer. They observe four Lents, as do the Greeks and most Eastern Christians; but it is said by Brerewood and Ross that they do not keep the Lord's day. There are three Coptic Liturgies: one attributed to St. Basil, another to St. Gregory, and the third to St. Cyril. These are translated into Arabic for the use of the clergy and the people.

The Copts are fond of rites and ceremonies. During the time of service they are always in motion, in particular the officiating priest is in continual motion, incensing the saints, pictures, books, &c., every moment; a traveller states *that* "many of their responses are made to the clanging of cymbals." They have many monasteries, in which the monks bury themselves from society in remote solitudes. Their nunneries are properly hospitals, and few enter them except widows reduced to beggary.

THE MALAKANES.

The Malakanes, or True Believers, are so called from the Russian word *malaks*, milk, which is their food on fast days. The zeal of a Prussian prisoner of war first brought them into notice in the middle of the last century. He settled in a village under the Government of Kharkow, and spent his life in explaining the Scriptures to the villagers, and visiting from house to house. After his death they began to look upon him as the founder of their sect, though it seems more probable that he only revived the Scriptural doctrines he found still lingering in the Russian Church.

They acknowledge the Bible as the Word of God, and the Trinity as the Godhead. They *admit the fall* of Adam and the resurrection of *our Lord.* They maintain that Adam's soul only, and not his body, was made after God's image. The Ten Commandments are received among them. Idolatry and the worship of images are forbidden. It is considered sinful to take an oath, and the observance of the Sabbath is strictly enjoined; so much so that, like many of the Oriental sects, they devote Saturday evening to preparation for the Sabbath. They are firm believers in the Millennium, and are improperly described as the followers of the fanatical Terenti Beloreff, who was, in fact, a member of their body. He announced, in 1833, the coming of the Lord within two years and a half. Many Malakanes in consequence abandoned their callings and awaited the event in prayer and fasting. Beloreff persuaded himself that, like Elijah, he should ascend to heaven on a certain day in a chariot of fire. Thousands of his followers came from all parts of Russia to witness this miracle. Terenti appeared, majestically seated in a chariot, ordered the multitude to prostrate themselves, and then, opening his arms like an eagle spreading his wings, he leapt into the air, but dropping down on the heads of the gaping multitude, was instantly seized and dragged off to prison as an impostor. He died soon after, no doubt in a state of insanity, declaring himself to be the prophet of God. But many of the Russians still believe in his divine mission. A considerable number of his followers afterwards emigrated to Georgia, and settled in sight of Mount Ararat, expecting the Millennium. They spend whole days and nights in fasting and prayer, and have all their goods in common. Such delusions have frequently appeared in other countries, and may be expected sometimes to return. The sublime truths of revelation operating on a disordered mind, and there wrought up with incoherent fancies, naturally break out in some wild extravagance. It would be unjust to charge upon the Malakanes the follies of a demented fanatic.

MARTINISTS.

In the beginning of the present century the purest of the Russian sects arose under the *Chevalier St. Martin.* The efforts of the Martinists *were directed* chiefly to practical religion. By avoiding, as far as possible, religious disputes, and devoting themselves to works of benevolence and Christian morality, they soon gained extensive influence. At Moscow they founded a splendid library, accessible to all; deserving young men were provided with the means of studying in foreign universities, and their ranks were swelled by many of the greatest and best men in the empire. But the sudden growth of liberty of opinion roused the suspicions of the Empress Catherine. One of their most active leaders, Novikoff, was imprisoned, and others banished, and the library destroyed.

The Martinists were set free by the Emperor Paul. It is mentioned as an instance of his generosity that he wished to compensate Novikoff for his sufferings. Novikoff requested, as the only favour, the liberation of his fellow-prisoners in the same cause. The Martinists afterwards rose high in the esteem of the Emperor Alexander, and were frequently members of his council. For a short time they took a leading part in the affairs of Russia, and by *their* influence other religious societies were encouraged by the Government. But the policy of the late Emperor Nicholas was, on this, as on many other points, at variance with that of his elder brother; and the Martinists have met of late years with no encouragement. They have been improperly termed a sect: they had no singularities of creed or practice; they were rather a society for the promotion of Christianity, knowledge, and virtue, than a sect.

PHILLIPPONS.

The Phillippons, whose priests are old men, or stariki, are recruited from amongst young boys, whom their parents dedicate to this ministry in youth. As soon as the child's vocation is decided, he no more touches any animal food, renounces all strong drink, and remains unmarried all his life. The Phillippons fast on Wednesday, because it was the day on which Jesus was betrayed, and on Friday, in remembrance of his passion. They celebrate three extraordinary fasts,—The first, before Easter, continues seven weeks; the second, up to the commencement of August, fifteen days; and the third, before Christmas, which is prolonged six weeks. They cannot drink wine, except on special occasions. They cannot take an oath, but must substitute these words: "yes, yes, in truth," which they pronounce with a peculiar gesture of the hand. Many take no food but milk and vegetables. They are extremely abstinent. These sectarians resemble the disciples of Manicheism, who, supposing that matter is the source of all evil, strive to diminish it by ascetic vigour.

The Bypoportchine priests recognise no priestly hierarchy. They dislike the national bishops and priests so much that, when any one of them enters their houses, they hasten, so soon as they leave, to wash the seats and the walls. They believe that the church is in a period of decline and apostacy; that the true apostolic succession has been interrupted, and that legitimate priests are impossible at the present day. They await the coming of the Lord to reorganise the Church upon regular and holy foundations. "The world," they say, in their strange theology, "has had four eras—a spring or morning, from

Adam till the building of Solomon's Temple; a summer, or noon, which lasted till the birth of Christ; an autumn, or evening, until the appearance of the Antichrist, who came two hundred years ago; and now we are in the cold winter, the dark night which shall continue till the Lord will descend upon the earth to save men, and open their eyes to the true light."

RASCOLNIKS, OR SCHISMATICS.

The Rascolniks, or Schismatics, are divided into two great branches—those who have, and those who reject, a priesthood or clerical order. To the former belong the Starovertzi, or "those of the old faith." They have existed since 1659, when Nicon, a Russian patriarch, having corrected the liturgies, and introduced a few alterations in the ceremonies, many of the rustics protested against the change, and refused to submit to Nicon's innovations. Their points of difference are few, and for the most part frivolous. They use the old Sclavonic alphabet in their *liturgical books*; they make the sign of the cross *differently from* the parent church; the processions in their churches walk from right to left, instead of from left to right, as Nicon ordered. They think it unlawful to eat certain kinds of food, including hares and potatoes; and they prove from the Old Testament the unlawfulness of cutting their beards. They never celebrate the Eucharist, and only administer baptism at the approach of death. Under Peter the Great they suffered dreadful oppressions. They regard him as the Antichrist, and refer to his reign as the period when Satan was let loose amongst them.

Attempts have been lately made to reconcile them to the Church, which has met their prejudices so far as to declare that their prejudices do not amount to heresy. Their priests are even invited to receive ordination from the bishops of the established Church; and they are termed co-religionists; but these concessions are looked upon with suspicion. They have a great number of convents, governed by the same monastic rules as those in force in the Greek monasteries.

SKOPTZI, OR EUNUCHS.

The Skoptzi, or Eunuchs, bury their tenets in profound secresy. They have many followers amongst the tradesmen and jewellers of St. Petersburgh and other large towns. Their origin is unknown, but they entertain great reverence for the Emperor Peter III., the murdered husband of the Empress Catherine. They maintain that he was not murdered, but escaped to Siberia, and that the body of a soldier was buried instead! they believe Peter to have been a true emanation from Christ, and that, on his return, the great bell of Moscow will be tolled, and its sound will gather the true disciples from the remotest corners of the earth. Largesses and rewards are freely offered to those who join them. Whoever can succeed in making twelve converts is called an apostle. They are known by mysterious signs, and spend the night between Saturday and Sunday in performing their secret rites. It is known that they inflict upon themselves the most cruel tortures for the mortification of the flesh; for instance, their penances far exceed in severity even chains, iron crosses, and frequent scourgings. Hair-cloth garments are always worn next the skin. Many of these fanatics have died under the rigours of their self-inflicted torments.

A lower grade of these Eunuchs are the Khlisti, or Flagellants, who are victims of the same delusions. These are said to have a community of women. One of the great ceremonies of the Khlisti is to assemble in a room divested of every kind of furniture, and dance and leap about, while they strip themselves, occasionally bathing their heads and hands in a vase of water in the middle of the room, until they finally fall exhausted.

VOLUNTARY MARTYRS.

The Voluntary Martyrs, called Morelstschiki, seem, in embracing Christianity, to have retained many Pagan opinions, and resemble more the savage idolaters of Scandinavia than the disciples of the Gospel. Some of them, on an appointed day in each year, meet in a secret place, with a pit, filling it with wood, straw, and other combustible matter. The most zealous then descend into the burning pit, where they stoically burn to death, while their brothers applaud the saints who thus receive the baptism of fire. Others, without sacrificing life, cruelly mutilate their bodies, like the fanatics in India, who throw themselves beneath the triumphant car of their idol.

It is difficult to know what are the dogmas of these voluntary martyrs, because they have not printed books, and they do not confide to foreigners the mysteries of their sect. Regarding the Old and New Testament as having been corrupted, it is said that they give themselves the right to change it. They recognise God the Father, manifested to men under the double form of Jesus Christ and the Holy Ghost. They reject the true death and resurrection of Jesus, maintaining that the body placed in the sepulchre by Joseph of Arimathea was not the Lord's body, but that of an obscure soldier. They think that Christ will soon return and make his triumphant *entrance into* Moscow, and that thither his true *disciples* will rush from every part of the earth.

They do not observe the Sabbath. Their only religious ceremony is Easter. They then celebrate the Lord's Supper with bread which has been buried in the tomb of some saint, supposing that it thus receives a kind of mysterious consecration. Their meetings are held on Saturday night. The following are a few lines of one of their hymns.

"Be firm, mariners!
Triumph over the tempest!
Fear neither fire nor the whirlwind,
Christ is with us!
He will collect the faithful in his vessel;
His mast will not break!
His sails will never be rent!
And he will hold the helm firmly,
And land us in a safe haven.
The Holy Spirit is with us!
The Holy Spirit is with us!"

These sectarians are to be found in the north of Russia, in Siberia, and even upon the banks of the Volga. There are a few also at Moscow, St. Petersburgh, Riga, Odessa, &c. They try to make proselytes in the army; but the imperial police pursue their missionaries, and when they are discovered, punish them most severely.

DUNKERS (DIPPERS OR TUMBLERS).

ORIGIN.—This small society of German Baptists was founded by Conrad Peysel, a German, at Euphrata, within fifty miles of Philadelphia, in 1724.

PROGRESS.—In 1777 their numbers did not exceed five hundred, but they soon formed a little colony called Euphrata, in allusion to the Hebrews, who used to sing psalms on the borders of the River Euphrates. They have since increased, but they are not now numerous.

The Dunkers are said to derive their name from baptizing by immersion, which they perform thrice; and as they presented themselves to the ordinance in a peculiar manner, bowing forward, they were in ridicule called "Tumblers."

TENETS.—The Dunkers are said to hold the leading tenets of the Universalists, and to possess the Quakers' scruples in regard to resistance, *war, slavery*, and litigation, on which account *they have* been called "The harmless Dunkers."

RITES AND CEREMONIES. — They practise trine immersion. Their rule is monastic, the men and women having separate habitations and distinct governments; but those who are disposed to marry are allowed to do so, and to preserve their connection with the society, but must remove from the settlement.

The Dunkers abstain from eating flesh except upon particular occasions, and observe in other respects a monkish austerity, believing in the expiatory efficacy of penance and mortification of the body. The men wear a dress similar to that of the Dominican friars.

EPISCOPALIANS (SCOTTISH).

ORIGIN.—The Reformation, which began to dawn on Scotland in 1527, made its way in the midst of great tumult and confusion. At length, "The Lords (or Leaders) of the Congregation," which was the name assumed by the Reformers in 1557, disliking the name much more than the reality of Episcopacy, set up a resemblance to it *in 1560*, projected by the celebrated John Knox, *under* the name of a "Superintendency."

PROGRESS. — In 1560, the Reformation in Scotland received the sanction of Parliament; and in 1567, it was sanctioned by the executive government. The form of church polity that had been established by John Knox having failed, a new form was adopted in 1572, when the Name of Episcopacy was resumed, together with almost everything that was necessary to constitute its reality, except the consecration of bishops.

This improved, but still defective, constitution of the church did not long continue; and the Reformers, after a struggle of five years, condemned it as both unlawful and unscriptural; they made nearer approaches to Presbyterianism, and through the influence of Mr. Andrew Melville, who was a great promoter if not the parent, of Scottish Presbyterianism, it was at last adopted and established by Act of Parliament in 1592. In this state, or nearly so, the church continued till the accession of King James to the Crown of England in 1603. He, in 1610, constituted a regular Episcopal Church, investing it with episcopal powers and authorities.

The spirit of rebellion, which had fermented during the life of James, broke out into open rupture in the reign of his son Charles, and the church was again thrown into confusion. "A solemn league and covenant" was entered into in 1638, for effecting the entire extirpation "of the government of the church by archbishops and bishops," &c.

The rights of both Monarchy and Episcopacy were trampled upon by these Covenanters, and the long period of tyranny and persecution that followed, brought the Episcopal succession in Scotland to almost total extinction. On the restoration of monarchy in the person of Charles II., the restoration of Episcopacy was resolved upon, and in January, 1662, it was publicly announced by the Privy Council, and confirmed in the next session of the Scottish Parliament, with only one dissenting voice.

At the Revolution, the Church of Scotland was once more doomed to destruction. Her bishops and clergy conceived their allegiance as due to James II., and that it could never be dissolved but by his death, and therefore refused the oaths of allegiance and assurance to King William, and afterwards the oath of abjuration; from which circumstance they obtained the name of "Nonjurors."

Episcopacy was now voted a grievance to the nation, and was abolished by the King and Parliament. Some relaxations of the severities with which the clergy were treated by King William were granted them by Queen Anne in 1712, and public chapels, which had till then been prohibited, were everywhere built and frequented, and in 1720 their congregations were as numerous as heretofore. In 1746 and 1748 severe prohibitory and penal statutes were enacted, in consequence of the avowed attachment of the Episcopalians to the House of Stuart, another attempt being then made to reinstate that family on the throne of their ancestors.

The death of Prince Charles Edward having occurred in 1792, these laws were wholly repealed, and the Scottish Episcopalians were tolerated like other dissenters from the national *establishment*, on which footing they have *remained* ever since.

The Episcopalians are the only society of dissenters from the establishment in Scotland that has yet been publicly recognized by law. Their clergy amount to more than eighty, and average nearly the same number of congregations, the members of which are supposed not to exceed 50,000.

TENETS.—They subscribe to the Thirty-nine Articles of the Church of England, and may be ranked, with scarcely an exception, as anti-Calvinists.

THE GREEK CHURCH.

ORIGIN.—The following ingenious argument relative to the great antiquity of this church emanates from the pen of a learned divine of the present day:—"The Oriental or Greek Church is the most ancient of all Christian churches, as it cannot be doubted that the first Christian church or society was established at Jerusalem. The prophet Isaiah says, 'The law went out of Zion, and the word of the Lord from Jerusalem.' *This city* was the mother of all churches, the original emporium of the Christian faith; the centre from which the healing rays of Christianity diverged and spread over the world."

The GREEK Church is so called from its comprehending all Christians within the limits of ancient Greece, and also from its members having long universally used the Greek language in its liturgies or religious services,—a practice they still continue, to distinguish it from the LATIN or Romish Church.

PROGRESS.—The Greek and Latin Churches, for the first eight centuries, were in communion with one another, although they disagreed in some points. In the ninth century, their disputes ran so high that a final separation took place between them, and each remains to this day the centre of a different system.

Little further remains to be related concerning the Greek Church, excepting the Crusades or Holy Wars, and the vast accession that was made to it in the fifteenth century by Prince Wladimir, who compelled several Sclavonian nations, and *especially the* Russians, to adopt the creed of the *Greek Christians.*

In 1543, when the Turks, under Mohammed the Second, took Constantinople, and overthrew the Grecian Empire, under the last of the Byzantine Cæsars, their religious establishment was overthrown also; and, though a partial toleration was at first permitted persecution soon reduced the Christian religion and its professors to the miserable state in which, for so many years, they existed under the yoke of the Ottomans.

The Greeks, under the present Turkish Government, are allowed to build no new churches, have to pay dearly for the permission to repair the old ones; are not allowed to have steeples or bells to their churches, nor even to wear the Turkish dress. They generally perform their religious service by night; moreover, they are obliged to pay tolls from which the Turks are free; and the males also pay to the Sultan after their fifteenth year a heavy poll-tax, under the significant name of "Exemption from beheading."

The most recent computations give the number of those Christians who are comprehended in the communion of the Greek church as 50,000,000 in Russia; 12,000,000, in Turkey,

Greece, including the Montenegrins, 800,000; the Austrian dominions. 2,800,000 ; the Patriarchate of Alexandria, 5,000 ; Antioch, 150,000 ; and Jerusalem, 15,000 ; in all about 65,500,000.

TENETS.—The Greek Church acknowledges as the rule of its faith the Holy Scriptures, and the decrees of the first seven General Councils ; but no private person has a right to explain for himself or others either the declarations of Scripture or the decisions of these Councils.

The Nicene and the Athanasian Creeds are allowed by them, and they hold the doctrine of the Trinity, but with this qualification, that the Holy Ghost proceeds from the Father only, and not from the Father and the Son.

RITES AND CEREMONIES.—They use what is called *trine* immersion in baptism, that is, they dip the person three times under water in the name of the Father, the Son, and the Holy Ghost. When the child is baptized, the priest anoints it with the *holy chrism*, which is applied to the forehead, eyes, nostrils, mouth, ears, breast, hands, and feet.

Extreme Unction is practised in some degree ;

but they disclaim that name, calling it the *Euchelaion*, or mystery of the holy oil. It is administered to all sick persons as often as such persons desire it, without waiting till the sick person is at the point of death; nor is it deemed essential to salvation.

They strictly abstain from eating things strangled, and such other meats as are prohibited in the Old Testament.

In the observance of divine fasts and feasts, the Greek Christians are rigid and superstitious; particularly as to the Lents, of which they have four every year. At these times they eat nothing that has blood, or oil, nor milk-meats, but herbs and shell-fish; and are so extremely particular and strict as scarcely to allow an egg or flesh-broth to a sick person.

GREEK CHURCH (RUSSIAN).

ORIGIN.—Christianity, it is supposed, was first introduced into Russia about the year 995, when it was professed by the Princess Olga, who was baptized at Constantinople. She recommended it to her grandson Vladimir, on whose baptism in 998 it was adopted by the nation generally, and from that time the Greek Church has been the established religion throughout this vast empire.

PROGRESS. — During the middle ages, the doctrine of Transubstantiation and other tenets peculiar to the Romish Church were covertly introduced; and by the irruption of the Mongol Tartars in the fifteenth century, an entire stop was put to learning, civilization, and religion for full two centuries.

On the accession of the present dynasty in 1613, the useful arts of life revived, Christianity was restored, and schools were established for the education of the Russian clergy.

The Patriarch of Russia was formerly almost equal to the Czar himself. Peter the Great, on the death of the Patriarch in 1700, abolished his office, and, having declared himself head of the National Church, appointed an Exarch .In 1721 he abolished this office also, and appointed "A Holy Legislative Synod," consisting of a council, *which he* established at St. Petersburgh. He also deprived the clergy of nearly all their rich endowments. But it was left for the Empress Catherine to annihilate the power of the clergy, and to complete their impoverishment. She appropriated the whole of the immoveable property of the church and clergy to the use of the Crown, appointing stipends in exchange to the monasteries and their rulers.

The Russian Church is still nominally governed by the Holy Synod, though really by the Czar. It is usually composed of two Metropolitans, two Bishops, the chief secular priest of the Imperial Staff, and the following lay members: the Procurator, two chief and five under secretaries, and a certain number of clerks.

The Procurator has the right of suspending its decisions for the Emperor's approval. From recent returns the number of the Russian clergy of all ranks averages about 220,000. The Russian Church Service is in the Sclavonic tongue, and occupies upwards of twenty volumes folio.

TENETS.—This church agrees almost in every point of doctrine with the Greek Church, to which article the reader is referred.

Rites and Ceremonies.—In addition to the forms and services of the Greek Church, most of which the Russians have always used, they still retain various ceremonies and superstitions of their own.

The Russians, with the Mother Church, have four Lents annually, besides a great number of abstinences or fasts; and Wednesdays and Fridays, which are fish-days throughout the whole year. The *first* Lent comprehends the forty days previous to Christmas; the *second*, which is their great Lent, the same space of time before Easter; the *third*, called the Lent of St. Peter, commences the week after Pentecost, or Whitsunday, and ends on the feast of St. Peter, June 29th; and the *fourth*, the Lent of the Mother of God, begins on the 1st and ends on the 15th of August, which is the day of *Koimesis*, or the Assumption of the blessed Virgin.

HUGUENOTS (OR FRENCH PROTESTANTS).

Origin.—During the reign of Francis I., in

1515, the principles of those great reformers, Luther and Zuinglius, first gained an entrance into France.

The term of "Huguenot" is of uncertain origin: one explanation derives it from a gate in Tours, called "*Hugon*," where the Protestants first assembled; another from the first words of their original protest, "*Huc nos.*"

PROGRESS.—Although Francis endeavoured to suppress the doctrines of Calvin by penal laws, the Huguenots increased, and under his successor Henry II. they made a further progress. This intolerant monarch adopted a cruel line of policy, his parliament at Paris sanctioning an edict by which the Huguenots were placed out of the protection of the law, and liberty granted to every Roman Catholic to destroy them. Their cause, however, still triumphed: they not only began to form religious assemblies, but were soon able to establish numerous churches in the capital and in the provinces.

They had undergone every variety of persecution, when the massacre at Paris, on the eve of St. Bartholomew (August 24, 1572), perpetrated under the feeble reign of Charles IX., filled all Protestant Europe with horror, upwards of 70,000 Huguenots being butchered on that occasion. Their sufferings were but slightly mitigated until Henry IV., who tolerated and protected them during his reign; passed in their favour, in 1598, the famous Edict of Nantes, whereby they were allowed the free exercise of their religion, and were admitted to various civil as well as ecclesiastical privileges. This edict was revoked in 1685, during the minority of Louis XIV., when the persecution again began; their churches were demolished, their estates confiscated, and, after the loss of innumerable lives, finally 500,000 Huguenots fled to Switzerland, Germany, Holland, and England, notwithstanding every part of the French frontiers was guarded with the utmost vigilance.

In the reign of Louis XV., new but less sever measures were adopted against the Protestants, and in 1746 they ventured to appear publicly in Languedoc and Dauphiny. In 1762, Protestant were no longer molested; yet they did not dare to make pretensions to public offices.

The Revolution restored them to all their civil rights, and during the reign of Buonaparte they frequently laid out their hitherto secreted treasures in the purchase of the national domains.

Although they did not offer any opposition to the new order of things, which took place on the restoration of the Bourbons, disturbances attended with bloodshed took place at Nismes and the vicinity, which were speedily suppressed by the judicious measures of government.

The pastors of all Christian communities in France are paid by the state. Protestant pastors are now paid, on account of their wives and families, at the rate of about £56 per annum each, which is more than is allowed to the Roman Catholic clergy. This stipend is considered to constitute only two-thirds of the provision for the several pastors, who are expected to get the remainder from their respective flocks.

Tenets.—Their confession of faith, which has received the approbation and the signatures of the most illustrious of the friends of the Reformation in France, is Calvinistic.

The Church of Geneva, to which all the Reformed in France were united by their doctrine, became also the model for their church polity and discipline.

INDEPENDENTS.

Origin.—This sect, which Puritanism gave birth to, was first formed in Holland in 1610.

They derive their name from maintaining that each congregation of Christians, which meets ordinarily in one place for public worship, is a complete church, has full power to regulate everything relating to religious government within itself, and is in no respect dependent upon or accountable to other churches.

Progress.—During the seventeenth century, at Leyden, at Middleburgh, and at Rotterdam, were numerous churches of English exiles, who had adopted the views of church-fellowship and government which have since distinguished the body of English Independents.

The founder of the sect, as it now stands, is allowed to have been Mr. John Robinson, of *Norfolk; he,* meeting with Mr. Henry Jacob in

Holland, and their sentiments on church discipline coinciding, Mr. Jacob returned to England about 1616, and established the first Independent church there.

The Independents were a very considerable body till the troubles in the reign of Charles I.; then, as Episcopacy began to decline, they became more considerable both in numbers and reputation. During the administration of Cromwell, who, for political purposes, bestowed on them his protection and patronage, they acquired a vast influence; but after the Restoration their cause declined, and they gradually sunk into obscurity; continuing to decline till 1691, in the reign of King William, when they entered into an association with the Presbyterians, comprised in nine articles, that tended to the maintenance of their respective institutions.

TENETS.—The creed of the Independents is uniformly Calvinistic, though with considerable shades of difference. That which distinguishes the Independents from every other sect is their maintaining that the power of church government, or discipline, is vested only in the community of the faithful at large; and their disclaiming every form of union between churches, and assigning to each congregation the exclusive government of itself; having full power within itself to admit and exclude members; to choose church officers, and to depose them without being accountable to any jurisdiction whatsoever.

INDEPENDENTS (SCOTTISH NEW).

Origin.—The churches composing this body, now associated under the name of "The Congregational Union of Scotland," for the most part originated in the labours of a society formed in 1797, under the auspices of Robert Haldane, Esq., for the avowed object of promoting the preaching of the gospel in those parts of Scotland devoid of evangelical instruction.

Mr. Haldane had sold his estates with the intention of employing his fortune in diffusing among the tribes of Hindostan the arts of civilized life and the blessings of true religion; but, being thwarted in his plans by the jealous *restrictions of* government, he resolved to employ his fortune and exertions in propagating the gospel at home.

PROGRESS.—Acting upon this principle, Mr. James Haldane, brother of the above, Mr. Aikman, and others, traversed the greater part of Scotland, preaching to their countrymen, not without meeting considerable opposition, especially from the established clergy. They were soon succeeded by other labourers employed by the Society.

In a short time Messrs. Haldane separated from the Established Church, and shortly afterwards the Rev. Messrs. Innes and Ewing resigned their charges, and united themselves to the new society, which increased so greatly, that large places of public worship, distinguished by the name of "Tabernacles," were erected at Mr. R. Haldane's expense in the principal towns.

Mr. J. Haldane, with his congregation, Mr. Innes, and some others, subsequently embraced Baptist principles, which has occasioned a division in the body. The Congregationalists of Scotland have recently become more closely assimilated to their brethren in England, and, having rapidly increased in numbers, now form a very important and well-organized denomination. The number of churches comprised in the Congregational Union of Scotland (formed in 1812) amounted in 1836 to ninety-one.

TENETS.—Their doctrines are Calvinistical, and they reject all articles of faith, or creeds of human composition ; they insist that the Scriptures contain a full and complete model and system of doctrine, government, discipline, and worship, and that in them may be found an universal rule for the direction of Christians in their associated state, as well as all necessary instruction for faith and practice of individuals.

IRVINGITES.

As the followers of the late Edward Irving, notwithstanding the melancholy consciousness avowed by their master in his last moments of having laboured under a delusion, appear likely for a time to maintain their existence as a separate body, they claim a brief description.

ORIGIN.—This sect may attribute its origin *to the meetings* held in 1826, at Albury Park, at the invitation of the opulent proprietor, Henry Drummond, Esq. The ostensible object of these meetings was to inquire into the import of the unfulfilled prophecies relating to the restoration of the Jews and the millennium. It was not long, however, before the germs of those extravagances of opinion began to discover themselves, which afterwards became the distinguishing and prominent characteristic of Mr. Irving's followers.

PROGRESS.—A spirit of gross fanaticism, resulting, from religious controversies, had exhibited itself at Gairloch, in Ross-shire. From what was supposed to be her dying bed, a young woman, named Mary Campbell, in 1830, at Fernicary, addressed her visitors with a fervour and fluency which appeared to them preternatural, and which she was herself led to ascribe to inspiration. Contrary to all expectation, she began to recover; and, with the prospect of returning health, she resolved to devote her future life to the conversion of the heathen. Conceiving herself specially called to the service, she prayed for the requisite qualifications, and, in answer, received, as she supposed, the gift of speaking in unknown tongues, and writing in unknown characters, although the gift of understanding, or interpreting the language uttered, was withheld: to this imaginary endowment was soon added a pretension to the power of working miracles!

It was not long before the scene of these miraculous pretensions was transferred to the English metropolis, and the "Gifts" were now confined to the congregation of the Rev. Edward Irving, then a minister of the Scottish Kirk.

Those individuals who conceived themselves to have received "The Gift of Tongues," soon assumed also that of prophecy, uttering their warnings professedly under the constraining influence of a supernatural power, partly in what they called "The Tongue," and partly in English. "The Tongue" burst forth from the gifted person so suddenly, and with such loud and rapid vociferation, that the hearer could scarcely recover from the shock before the English commenced. Some spoke for two hours and upwards, with very little interval, giving forth prophecies concerning the church and the nation.

These performances having continued nearly eighteen months, it was thought proper to bring Mr. Irving's notions under the cognizance of the Judicatories of the Scottish Church. Accordingly, in March, 1833, he was tried by the Presbytery of Annan, and suspended from his office as a minister of the national church.

On the morning upon which he was, in pursuance of this sentence, shut out of his church in Regent-square, he pronounced a curse upon the place, and declared that it should never again prosper. A new and elegant chapel was subsequently opened and consecrated, in Newman-street, Oxford-street. On the same night he presented his infant child for baptism, and gave it the name of "Ebenezer," in token that the Lord had thus far helped him. In a short time the child sickened, and, when it was dying, the prophets and elders were summoned into the chamber, when one of the gifted persons declared it to be the will of the Lord that the child should not die! While they were in the act of praying, and commanding it to revive, it expired! upon which another manifestation burst fort.

that it was the will of the Lord it should be restored to life. But the spirit would not come again at their bidding, and the child was entombed under the very church which its father had a short time before cursed.

On being summoned to appear before the General Assembly, Mr. Irving repaired to Scotland; but, instead of waiting to receive the sentence passed upon his errors, he stood up, and angrily denounced his judges, declaring that the fearful judgment of God would fall upon them for resisting the work he was engaged in, and so left them, still upheld in his delusion by the assurances of his prophets. Very shortly afterwards he was seized with fever, and the fatal symptoms of consumptive malady. In spite of confident predictions to the contrary, he expired in the land which he was to have astonished with his power; and his remains repose under one of the churches, the ministers of which he had threatened with awful judgments. He died at Glasgow, Dec. 6th, 1834, in his thirty-fourth year.

"*Besides*," (says Mr. Josiah Conder, to whose

"View of all Religions, 1838," we are indebted for this article), "the principal chapel in Newman-street, the Irvingites have (or had) six others, in and near London, named after 'The Seven Churches of Asia,' and having their apostles, and pillars of apostles; prophets, and pillars of prophets; angels, and pillars of angels; elders, evangelists, &c., &c. As their meetings are for the most part private, little is known of what takes place at them. Mr. Drummond is the angel of the church at Albury, from which the husband of Mary Campbell, Mr. Caird, was sent forth as an Evangelist. He afterwards presided over a church gathered under the episcopal auspices of Mr. Drummond, at Brighton. A foreign mission also has been undertaken by some members of the society, in emulation of the proceedings of the 'Early Friends.' What is not a little remarkable, some members of the society of 'Friends' have embraced the tenets of the Irvingites, which rest upon claims to immediate inspiration, strikingly similar to those that form the basis of Quakerism."

LUTHERANS.

This sect are so named from their being followers of the doctrines of MARTIN LUTHER, an Augustine Friar, who was born in upper Saxony, in 1483, one of the most intrepid and most successful of reformers.

ORIGIN.—Luther first took offence at the indulgences which were granted in 1517, by Pope Leo X., to those who contributed towards finishing St. Peter's Church at Rome, Luther being then professor of divinity at Wittemburg. Those indulgences promised remission of all sins, past, present, and to come, however enormous their nature, to all who were rich enough to purchase them. At this Luther raised his warning voice, and publicly at Wittemburg he exposed the traffic in indulgences, and subsequently attacked the supremacy of the Pope. This was the commencement of that memorable revolution in the Church, which is styled the REFORMATION.

PROGRESS.—In 1520, Luther and his partisans *were excommunicated*; when this great reformer, whom diligent researches into the Scriptures had convinced of the errors of the Church of Rome, immediately and publicly renounced her communion.

After appearing at the Diet of Worms in 1521, which he left a conqueror, it became so manifest that his enemies were determined on his destruction, that Frederic the Wise conveyed him privately to the castle at Wartzburg, where he was concealed nine months, during which he translated the New Testament into German, encouraging his adherents by his pen, and being cheered in return by receiving accounts of the rapid diffusion of his doctrines. In the same year Luther entered the lists of controversy with King Henry VIII.; and it was the disputes and attacks that followed, that matured his plans for a total reformation in the Church, which he conceived to be imperatively called for.

In 1523 he began to purify the Liturgy from its empty forms, and by laying aside his cowl in 1524, he gave the signal for the abolition of the monasteries. In 1525 he married Catherine Von Bora, a nun. This he did, as much from principle as inclination, with the design of restoring the preachers of the gospel to their natural and social rights and duties.

From 1526 to 1529 Luther prepared a new church service, with the aid of Melancthon and other members of the Saxon church; also catechisms to be used in schools. In 1527 John, the Elector of Saxony, took a decisive step, and established the Lutheran religion throughout his dominions, as did Philip, Landgrave of Hesse. In 1529, at the Diet of Worms, a suspension of a decree against the Lutherans was revoked through the influence of Charles V. Against this *new* decree six princes and the deputies of thirteen imperial cities and towns solemnly *protested*, and from this the appellation of PROTESTANTS became common to all who embraced the Lutheran and reformed religion.

At the Diet of Augsburg, in 1530, the reformers presented their confession of faith and practice; and hence it obtained the name of the Confession of Augsburg. The Reformation was now gaining ground with inconceivable rapidity *in most* of the countries of Europe. Within the space of five or six years it spread from Hungary and Bohemia to France and England; then to Sweden and Denmark; and, subsequently, to Brandenburg, Pomerania, Mecklenburg, Holstein, &c.

On the death of Luther, which occurred in 1546, Philip Melancthon, the Greek Professor at Wittemburg, was placed at the head of the Lutheran Church. It now became a prey to intestine disputes, which continued more or less until the end of the sixteenth century; the disciples of Calvin soon separating from the church. In the seventeenth century the principles of the Lutheran Church were carried into Asia, Africa, and America, and were also introduced into some parts of Europe where they had hitherto been unknown.

Lutheranism is now the established or prevailing form of the Protestant faith in Saxony, Prussia, Wittemburg, Hanover, and great part of Northern Germany, in Denmark, Sweden, and Norway. There are also Lutheran churches in Holland, Russia, Poland, and Hungary, and in the United States of America. Of sixteen Protestant Universities in Germany, fourteen are Lutheran. In France the Lutherans have about two hundred and fifty congregations.

TENETS.—The members of this church are distinguished principally by the following doctrines:—That neither the Pope nor any other man possesses any authority in matters of faith, but that the Scriptures are, as a collection of inspired, sufficient, and clear writings, the only source whence our religious sentiments, whether they relate to faith or practice, must be drawn, and to which human reason ought, in every respect, to submit and yield; that man is naturally incapable of thinking or doing any good, valid before God; that justification and future happiness are the effect of the meritorious and vicarious death of Jesus, as God and man in one person; that faith is the necessary condition of grace on the part of man, which faith is itself the gift of divine grace; that good works are of value only as far as they are the effect of faith; that, however, there exists no unconditional predestination; and that the real body and blood of Jesus are united *in a mysterious* manner, through the consecration, with the bread and wine, and are received *with and under* them in the sacrament of the Lord's Supper. This last doctrine they distinguish by the word *Consubstantiation;* and it formed, together with the doctrine of predestination, for a long time, the principal "party wall" between the Lutherans and Calvinists; but it, as well as some of the other doctrines, has been, if not formally, at least almost virtually abandoned, or considerably modified, by a great number of Lutherans.

METHODISTS (ARMINIAN, OR WESLEYAN).

Origin.—This body of Christians owe their origin to the Methodist Society, which was first founded at Oxford, in 1729. Mr. John Wesley, then a fellow and tutor at Lincoln College, Mr. Charles Wesley, a student and tutor of Christ Church, and two other commoners, set apart some evenings in the week for reading the Greek Testament, religious conversation, and prayer. In 1732 they were joined by others of the same serious dispositions; and in 1735, by the celebrated Mr. George Whitfield, of Pembroke College, then in his eighteenth year.

The name of *Methodists* was bestowed upon them by their more worldly fellow-students, on account of their methodical observance of the rules of religion and the regularity of their lives. This name was also adopted by themselves, and has since been continued to their followers.

Progress.—In 1735, Messrs. John and Charles Wesley sailed for Georgia, in order to preach the Gospel to the Indians. While Mr. John Wesley was employed at Savannah, several circumstances of a disagreeable nature occurred, which induced him to return to England, after an absence of two years, when he was succeeded by Mr. Whitfield.

Mr. Wesley having resumed his ministry in England, his labours were attended with great success. Many appeared to be religiously impressed, and disposed to meet together for spiritual conversation and prayer. Accordingly, in 1738, he formed them into a society in London, which held its conferences in a private house, *without* any disposition at this time to secede from the Church; but the clergy of the Establishment having refused him their pulpits, he preached in Newgate, in some Dissenting chapels in London, and in different places in the country where he could gain admission. Multitudes still crowding from all quarters to hear him, he was at length compelled to take the open air and become field-preacher. This was the origin and commencement of his itinerancy.

In 1741, the Rev. George Whitfield returned to England. During the period of his labours in America he had imbibed certain doctrines contrary to those taught by Mr. Wesley, and a separation took place.

Mr. Wesley, finding his societies increasing very fast in London, Bristol, and other places, was induced to select from his followers those whom he judged the best qualified to instruct the rest. This was the origin of his "Lay Preachers." Having now abundance of assistants, pious, zealous, and active, he sent them forth in every direction; some to watch over the Societies already formed, and others to the highways to preach to the most dissolute and abandoned. In every part of the kingdom their labours were eminently useful, numerous Societies being formed. They did not, however, labour without molestation. In many places they were beset by mobs, and assailed with showers of stones, and sometimes persecuted with the most unrelenting cruelty. Methodism, however, soon rose above the opposition of its foes, and overspread the country.

Since that period to the present time its numbers have been steadily and rapidly increasing in every part of the United Kingdom; so much so, that the Wesleyan Methodists of all classes average 30,000 congregations, and 1,460,000 attendants.

TENETS.—I. The Wesleyan Methodists maintain the total fall of man in Adam, and his utter inability to recover himself, or take one step towards his recovery, "without the grace of God assisting him, that he may have a good will, and working with him, when he has that good will."

II. They hold general redemption. They assert "that Christ, by the grace of God, tasted *death for* every man." This grace they call "*free*," as extending itself freely to all.

They hold justification by faith. "This justification," says Mr. Wesley, "signifies present forgiveness, pardon of sins, and consequently acceptance with God, who therein declares his righteousness or justice and mercy, by, or for the remission of the sins that are past, saying, I will be merciful to thy unrighteousness, and thine iniquities I will remember no more. I believe the condition of this is faith (Rom. iv. 5, &c.); I mean not only that without faith we cannot be justified, but, also, that as soon as any one has true faith, in that moment he is justified. Justifying faith implies not only a divine evidence, or conviction that God was in Christ, reconciling the world unto himself, but a sure trust and confidence that Christ died for my sins; that he loved me, and gave himself for me. And the moment a penitent sinner believes this, God pardons and absolves him."

IV. They hold the witness of the Spirit. Mr. Wesley says: "The testimony of the Spirit is an inward impression on the soul, whereby the Spirit of God directly witnesses to my spirit that I am a child of God; that Jesus Christ hath loved me, and given himself for me; that all my sins are blotted out, and I am reconciled to God. The *manner* how the divine testimony is manifested to the heart I do not take upon me to explain. But the fact we know, namely, that the Spirit of God does give a believer such a testimony of his adoption, that while it is present to the soul, he can no more doubt the reality of his sonship than he can doubt the shining of the sun while he stands in the full blaze of his beams."

V. They maintain that, by virtue of the blood of Jesus Christ, and the operations of the Holy Spirit, it is their privilege to arrive at that maturity in grace, and participation of the divine nature, which excludes sin from the heart, and fills it with perfect love to God and man. This they denominate "Christian perfection."

RITES AND CEREMONIES. — *Class Meetings* are each composed of from twelve to twenty persons, one of whom is styled the leader. When they assemble, which is once a week, the leader gives out a few verses of a hymn, which they join in singing. He then makes a short *prayer*, after which he converses with each member respecting Christian experience, gives suitable advice to all, and concludes by singing and praying.

Band Meetings consist of about four or five members, who are nearly of the same age, in nearly similar circumstances, and of the same sex, who meet together once a week in order to speak their minds more freely than it would be agreeable to do in a promiscuous assembly of members, such as a class-meeting. At stated periods, those who meet in these private bands, meet all together, forming a public or select band, when, after singing and prayer, any of the members are at liberty to rise and speak their experience. After a few of them have spoken, the meeting, as usual, is concluded by singing and prayer.

Watch-nights are rather similar to the vigils of the ancients, which they kept on the evenings preceding the grand festivals. They are held once a quarter. On these occasions, three or four of the preachers officiate, and a great concourse of people attend. The service commences between eight and nine at night. After one of the ministers has preached, the rest pray and exhort, giving out at intervals suitable hymns, which the congregation join in singing till a few minutes after twelve o'clock, when they conclude.

Love-feasts are also held quarterly. No persons are admitted who cannot produce a ticket to show that they are members, or a note of admittance from the superintendent. However, any serious person, who has never been present at one of these meetings, may be supplied with a note for once, but not oftener, unless he becomes a member. The meeting begins with singing and prayer. Afterwards small pieces of bread, or plain cake, and some water, are distributed; and all present eat and drink together in token of their Christian love to each other. Then, if any persons have anything particular to say concerning their present Christian experience, or the manner in which they were first brought to the knowledge of the truth, they are permitted to speak; when a few of them have spoken, a collection is made for the poor, and the meeting is *concluded* with singing and prayer.

METHODISTS (AMERICAN WESLEYAN).

ORIGIN.—The first Methodist society was established in New York, 1766, by preachers from Ireland.

PROGRESS. — Their numbers increased so rapidly, that in 1768 they erected a meeting-house. Several preachers were soon after sent out from England, and the first conference was held at Philadelphia in 1773. During the war, all the English preachers returned home, except Mr. Asbury. At the close of the Revolution in 1784, Mr. Wesley sent out Dr. Coke, with directions to consecrate Mr. Asbury superintendent or bishop of the American Church, which was done at Baltimore; twelve of the preachers were at the same time ordained elders.

The form of government is Episcopal. Three orders of ministers are recognised — deacons, elders, and bishops.

The whole number of members, in 1853, scattered over an immense tract of country, were placed under the care of 28 conferences, and superintended by six bishops. There were 3,100 itinerant ministers; 2,220 who were superannuated; and 5,800 local preachers. The private members amounted to 686,549; of whom 605,212 were white; 79,236 were coloured; and 2,101 were Indians.

The number of hearers who attend Methodist preaching throughout the United States is averaged at more than 1,000,000. All the Methodists in this country are Wesleyans.

WESLEYAN NEW CONNEXION (OR KILHAMITES).

Origin.—The grounds of this separation, which took place in 1797, are, that in the latter part of his life Mr. Wesley thought proper to assume the Episcopal office, and not only to ordain several ministers, who were sent out to Scotland and to America, but also to consecrate some as bishops.

During his lifetime some of the Societies petitioned to have preaching in their own chapels in church hours, which was contrary to his original directions; and to have the Lord's *Supper* administered by the travelling preachers.

This request he generally refused to comply with; and where it could be conveniently done, he sent some of the clergymen, who officiated at the New Chapel, London, to perform these sacred offices.

After his decease in 1791, the same request was renewed by many of the Societies; when they had the mortification to find that this question was decided against them by lot. The subject still continued to be agitated; and the dissatisfaction occasioned by the decisions of Conference, together with some other differences, led, in 1797, to the secession of a considerable body, who form what is termed the "Methodist New Connexion." Sometimes they are called "Kilhamites," from their most prominent leader, the Rev. Alexander Kilham.

The New Methodists differ from the Old Methodists in the more popular constitution of their church government; the preachers and the lay-deputies chosen by the people being associated in all meetings for business.

In 1855, the New Connexion numbered, in

Great Britain and Ireland, 83 preachers, and 16,884 members.

In Canada, which is divided into seven districts, there are 7,400 members.

METHODISTS (CALVINISTIC OR WHITFIELDITES),

ORIGIN.—About the year 1741, the two great Founders of Methodism, Mr. John Wesley and Mr. George Whitfield, entirely separated, in consequence of holding different opinions on the doctrines of free will and predestination.

Mr. Whitfield gave his whole attention to preaching, without attempting to organize a Sect, or to frame any system of discipline for his followers. He died in 1770, in the fifty-sixth year of his age, in Massachusetts, on his seventh missionary visit to America. His establishment in Georgia, where he had founded an orphan-house and academy, he bequeathed to Selina, Countess of Huntingdon, and his chapels in England were left to the management of trustees.

PROGRESS.—According to Dr. Haweis, Mr. *Whitfield's* followers in 1800 composed an aggregate nearly as numerous as the Wesleyan Methodists. In 1829, the total number of places of worship belonging to the Calvinistic Methodists amounted to 124. Although, comparatively speaking, not a very numerous body, they have in different parts of the United Kingdom a considerable number of preachers, whose congregations and the societies connected with them are very extensive: in Wales especially, the Calvinistic Methodists form a very numerous and compact class.

LADY HUNTINGDON'S CONNEXION.

A section of the Calvinistic Methodists still exists as a distinct body under the above name; consisting of the congregations assembling in the various chapels erected by Selina, Countess of Huntingdon, and vested in trustees.

Many of these in different parts of the country have, within the last fifty years, become severed from the connexion, in consequence of the difficulty of obtaining a succession of ministers, and have become Independent congregations.

Lady Huntingdon founded, in 1768, a college in South Wales for the purpose of educating young men for the ministry. After her death, in 1791, the Institution was transferred to Cheshunt, in Hertfordshire, where it still flourishes. The students are maintained and educated, entirely free, for four years. The number of chapels in England, in 1856, was 112; the number of attendants, according to the census, was more than 20,000.

MORAVIANS (OR UNITED BRETHREN).

Origin.—This Community derive their origin from the ancient Bohemian and Moravian Brethren, who existed as a distinct people ever since the year 1457; when, separating from those who took up arms in defence of their protestations against the eorors of Popery, they formed a plan for church-fellowship and discipline, agreeable to their insight into the Scriptures, and called themselves at firrst, "*Fratres Legis Christi;*" or Brethren after the Law of Christ.

Progress.—The fraternity were soon joined

by others of the same persuasion in other places, when they took the name "*Unitas Fratrum*," or *Fratres Unitatis*," (United Brethren). By degrees they established congregations in various places, and spread themselves into Moravia and other neighbouring states.

After suffering great persecutions, some emigrated to Silesia, and others into Upper Lusatia, a province of Saxony adjoining to Bohemia. The latter found a zealous protector in Count Zinzendorff, a Lutheran by education, and a man remarkable for his unaffected piety. He is very justly esteemed by them as the chief instrument in the hands of God in restoring their sinking church. He gave them some land on one of his estates in Upper Lusatia, upon which, in 1722, they built a village, and founded a colony. Count Zinzendorff is, in general, gratefully remembered for his disinterested and indefatigable labours in promoting the interests of religion, both at home and abroad. He died in 1760, in the 60th year of his age.

In 1742 and following years, they began establishments in England, and everywhere met with encouragement to develop their character and industrious habits. Thus their settlements were extended to North and South America, the West and East Indies, Russia, Asia, Africa, and Greenland, with a view to the propagation of the Gospel among the heathen.

The Moravian Episcopal succession, after mature investigation, was admitted by the Parliament of Great Britain, who acknowledged the "*Unitas Fratrum*" to be an ancient Protestant Episcopal Church, and passed an act in their favour in 1749.

The institutions of the Brethren at the present time consist of twenty-three settlements: of these, fourteen are in Germany and Holland; one in Russia; three in England; one in Ireland; and four in the United States, containing about 10,100 members; forty-five societies, and twenty or thirty smaller congregations, enumerating 86,300 members; and forty-five missionary stations, of which sixteen are regular settlements, occupying the labours of 116 missionaries. No religious community has done so much, in proportion to its members and limited resources, towards the diffusion of Christianity; and it is a distinguishing feature of the Moravian missions, that their labours have in every instance been directed to tribes on the extreme verge of civilization, or to the outcasts of humanity—the half-frozen Greenlander, the savage Esquimaux, and the despised Hottentot.

TENETS.—Though the Brethren acknowledge no other standard of truth than the Holy Scriptures, they in general profess to adhere to the Augsburg Confession of Faith. They teach the doctrine of the Trinity, nor do they differ in essentials from other Protestant Churches.

They profess to believe that the kingdom of Christ is not confined to any party, community, or church; and they consider themselves, though closely united in one body, or visible church, as spiritually joined in the bond of Christian love to all who are taught of God, and who belong to the universal Church of Christ, however much they may differ in forms, which they deem non-essentials.

RITES AND CEREMONIES. — All the great festivals celebrated in other Protestant Churches are attended to by the Moravians with due solemnity; and, during the whole of the passion-week, they have daily services for the contemplation of our Lord's last discourses and sufferings. On Maunday Thursday they celebrate the Lord's Supper, and also on every fourth Sunday throughout the year.

They have prescribed forms of prayer for baptisms both of children and adults, and for burials; a Litany, which is read every Sunday morning, and one for early service on Easter morning, besides others which they call Liturgies, and which are chiefly sung and chanted. Some of their services consist entirely in singing (the whole congregation joining), when a succession of verses forms a connected contemplation of some Scripture subject.

In marriage they may form a connexion with those only who are of their own communion. The brother who marries a person not of their congregation is considered as having quitted their church-fellowship. There is, however, no objection to a sister's marrying a person of approved piety in another communion; and some, by express licence, are permitted still to join in their church ordinances as before. A brother may make his own choice of a partner in the Society, and both parties may reject the proposals made to them; but, as all intercourse between the different sexes is less frequent among them than elsewhere, and few opportunities of forming particular attachments are found, they usually rather refer the choice to their friends and intimates than decide for themselves. As the lot must be cast to sanction their union, each receives his partner as a divine appointment; and, however strange this method may appear, there are, perhaps, nowhere fewer unhappy marriages to be found than among the Brethren.

In their settlements, at all hours, whether day or night, some persons of both sexes are appointed by rotation to pray for the Society.

MORMONITES (OR LATTER-DAY SAINTS).

Origin.—This sect first appeared in America, and Joseph Smith was its founder. He was born at Sharon, in the State of Vermont, in 1805, being the son of a small farmer. When about fifteen years of age he was present at one of those religious revivals which have become so frequent in some of the transatlantic churches.

Whether from insanity or sheer hypocrisy, the lad professed to have been favoured, while in prayer, with a miraculous vision. "A pillar of light above the brightness of the sun gradually descended upon me," he says, "and I saw two personages, whose brightness and glory defy all description, standing above me in the air." They assured him that his sins were forgiven, and forbade him to join any Christian church, since all existing churches were alike in error. His vanity led him to proclaim his vision, and the persecution which he says he met with, in consequence, from professors of religion, made him only the more obstinate. He admits that, as he grew up, he led a vagrant life. By the help of a divining-rod he pretended to be able to discover treasures buried in the earth, and was known as the "money-digger." He earned a precarious living by this and similar contrivances *till 1823*, when he had a second revelation, and an angel directed him to a spot near Palmyra, in Ontario county, where he found engraved on thin plates of gold certain records prophetic and historical. They were written in the "reformed Egyptian character," and had once belonged to the American Indians, who were a remnant of the Israelites; and they contained the necessary instructions for the formation of a pure church. Besides the record engraved on the gold plates, he found with them two stones or lenses, set in silver; these were the Urim and Thummim of the ancient seers, by means of which he was enabled to translate the book. It was not till 1827 that Smith was permitted by the angel to remove his treasure, though he continued to receive supernatural instructions during the interval. Such was Smith's declaration. In 1830 the Book was published under the title, "The Book of Mormon,"* pretended that it contained a

* According to Smith, Mormon was the name of a prophet who lived in the fourth century, and who engraved on plates of gold a summary of the history of the American tribes, which had now become degenerate and were soon afterwards extinct. These plates were buried for safety by his son Maroni, in the spot to which Smith was directed by the angel, about the year *A.D. 420.*

translation of the characters engraved upon the golden tablets, to which he had been directed by the angel.

As "The Book of Mormon" forbade infant baptism, Smith began to baptise a few of his converts, amongst whom were his own father and other members of his family. Soon afterwards Smith and his companions removed to a settlement on the banks of the Missouri, or City of Zion, and in 1832 the settlement was tenanted by no fewer than twelve hundred Mormonites. But the indignation of the old settlers was aroused, partly by the immoral practices which already began to be charged to the sect, and still more by their vaunts and arrogance; for they boasted they should soon possess the whole country, and that the infidels would be rooted out. A public meeting was held in the county, and the Mormonites were commanded to depart. Resistance was in vain. Nor could they obtain redress from the legal tribunals. Zion was abandoned, and the Mormonites, who now amounted to twelve thousand, crossed the Mis*sissippi,* in 1837, and took refuge in the State of

Illinois. Here they built Nauvoo, which, according to "The Book of Mormon," signifies beautiful.

Joseph Smith was shot June the 7th, 1848, in the thirty-ninth year of his age. His vacant office was eagerly contested by several competitors. "The Apostolic College" elected Brigham Young, who is now President of the Latter Day Saints, and of the territory of Utah. A mission had been sent to England, and already their tenets were making rapid progress. Within seven years they had baptised more than ten thousand British subjects.

The Mormon Creed, printed for general circulation, omits most of the questionable points both of their faith and practice. It is as follows:—

"We believe in God the eternal Father, and in his Son Jesus Christ, and in the Holy Ghost.

"We believe that men will be punished for their own sins, and not for Adam's transgressions.

"We believe that, through the atonement of

Christ, all mankind may be saved by obedience to the laws and ordinances of the Gospel.

"We believe that these ordinances are—1st. Faith in the Lord Jesus Christ. 2nd. Repentance. 3rd. Baptism by immersion, for the remission of sins. 4th. Laying on of hands for the gift of the Holy Spirit. 5th. The Lord's Supper.

"We believe that men must be called of God by inspiration, and by laying on of hands by those who are duly commissioned to preach the Gospel, and administered in the ordinances therefor

"We believe in the same organization that existed in the primitive Church, viz., apostles, prophets, pastors, teachers, evangelists, &c.

"We believe in the powers and gifts of the everlasting Gospel, viz., the gift of faith, discerning of spirits, prophecy, revelation, visions, healing, tongues, and the interpretation of tongues, wisdom, charity, brotherly love, &c.

"We believe in the Word of God, recorded in the Bible. We also believe the Word of God recorded in 'The Book of Mormon,' and in all *other good* books.

"We believe all that God has revealed, all that he does not reveal; and we believe that he will yet reveal many more great and important things pertaining to the kingdom of God and Messiah's second coming.

"We believe in the literal gathering of Israel, and in the restoration of the ten tribes; that Zion will be established upon the Western Continent; that Christ will reign personally upon the earth one thousand years; and that the earth will be renewed and receive its paradisiacal glory.

"We believe in the literal resurrection of the body, and that the dead in Christ will rise first, and that the rest of the dead live not again until the thousand years are expired.

"We claim the privilege of worshipping Almighty God, according to the dictates of our conscience, unmolested, and allow all men the same privilege, let them worship how or where they may.

"We believe in being subject to kings, queens, presidents, rulers, and magistrates, in obeying, honouring, and sustaining the law.

"We believe in being honest, true, chaste, temperate, benevolent, virtuous, and upright, and in doing good to all men; indeed, we may say that wefollow the admonition of Paul, "We believe all things,' 'we hope all things,' we have endured very many things, and hope to be able to 'endure all things.' Everything virtuous, lovely, praiseworthy, and of good report we seek after, looking forward to the recompense of reward."

In 1830, when Mormon baptism was instituted, and the only method of escape is by the vicarious substitution of a Mormon saint, who receives on their behalf what is termed "baptism for the dead." In this revelation, Smith has given explicit directions for the appointment of clerks or recorders to keep the books in the Mormonite temple at Nauvoo, in which the names of the deceased persons shall be entered on their behalf. Any living man receives "baptism for the dead." Notwithstanding the fair professions of benevolence and philanthropy in their creed, "The Book of Doctrines and Covenants" is filled *with bitter* denunciations against unbelievers, and revenge is inculcated as a duty. "And it shall come to pass that whosoever shall lay hands on you by violence, ye shall command to be smitten in my name, and behold I will smite them according to your words.

The doctrine of spiritual marriage is this:—No marriage is lawful without the sanction of the Mormon priesthood, by whom it may also be dissolved.

Polygamy is the privilege of the faithful and the Mahomedan paradise, with its sensual indulgences, is distinctly taught

PROGRESS.—Besides the great Mormon tribe, as they may be termed, in North California, the sect is now to be found in many states of Europe, in the Sandwich Islands, and in the East Indies. Its success has been great in England. The census reports 226 places of worship belonging to this body, most of them, however, being only rooms. The number of sittings in those places was about 30,000. From an official census of their own, we learn that the British Mormonites amount to 30,900. The number of those who bear office is a large proportion of the whole (about one in five).

and to this circumstance their success, no doubt, is much indebted. The officers of the Church in England numbered 40 seventies, 10 high priests, 2,590 elders, 1,940 priests, 1,587 teachers. and 962 deacons. The most numerous body in England is in Manchester, where the Mormon Church contains 3,284 members.

The excitable character of the Welsh peasantry has afforded some of its greatest triumphs to the Mormon cause; thousands have emigrated, but the Church at Merthyr Tydvil still contains 2,350 members.

NESTORIAN CHRISTIANS.

ORIGIN. — This sect take their name from Nestorius, a Syrian monk, who afterwards became a priest, and a preacher of great celebrity, and was at length, in 438, raised to the see of Constantinople.

PROGRESS.—The Nestorians formed so considerable a body that the Romanists exerted themselves to bring them under the Papal yoke, *and with this* view Innocent IV. in 1246, and

Nicholas III. in 1278, used their utmost endeavours, by means of Franciscan and Dominican missionaries, but without success. However, about the middle of the fifteenth century, these missionaries gained over to their communion a small number of Nestorians, whom they formed into a congregation or church. In the sixteenth century the Nestorians were divided into two sects, which separation has given rise to various factions, involving them in the greatest dangers and difficulties. That division has continued to the present day.

They are to be found scattered through Asia, also in some parts of the Levant; and it is recorded of them, that of all the Christian societies established in the East, the Nestorians have been the most careful and successful in avoiding a multitude of superstitions belonging to the Greek and Latin Churches.

TENETS. — The main points that distinguish the Nestorians from all other Christians are their believing that the Virgin Mary was *not* the Mother of Christ, as *God*, but only as *Man*:

and there were not only two *Natures*, but also two distinct *Persons*, in the Son of God.

PLYMOUTH BRETHREN.

ORIGIN.—The sect called Plymouth Brethren first appeared about the year 1830, in the town of Plymouth. There is some difficulty in laying before the reader, in a simple form, the principles of this body. It puts forth no standard of faith, nor publishes any form of worship or discipline. It professes to practise Christianity as it was taught by our Lord and the apostles in the New Testament. "The main peculiarity," they say, "which marks the position of those called 'Brethren,' is, that they desire to stand together in heart and in action upon God's ground for the union of his people; and consequently, in separation from all that, to their consciences, takes away this ground."

The Brethren equally object to the National Church, and to all forms of dissent or national churches, one and all of them. They say "that *the opening* of the door, to receive into the most solemn acts of worship and Christian fellowship the whole population of a country, is a latitudinarian error." Dissenters, on the other hand, "are sectarians, because they close the door on real Christians who cannot utter the Shibboleth of the party."

That which constitutes a church is the presence of the Holy Spirit. It is the owning of the Holy Ghost as Christ's Vicar—the really present, sole, and sufficient sovereignty in the Church during our Lord's absence, which is the leading feature in the testimony of the Brethren. From this position they draw two inferences.—First, that it is not by baptism, whether infant or adult—nor by the reception of any creed—but by the indwelling of the Holy Spirit, that any man becomes a member of the Christian Church; and, possessing this, he is a member of the Universal Church, not merely of any particular section of it; and he is entitled to all the privileges of communion with the Church Catholic throughout the world. Beyond this, all tests are sectarian, and ruinous to the church which imposes them; though the Brethren do not deny that, inasmuch as they contain amongst them those who are led by the Spirit of God, they may, in a certain sense, be churches still.

Secondly, that the government of the church is, if we, may be permitted the phrase, the monarchy of the Holy Ghost. He abideth within his church and governs it. All ecclesiastical appointments are made by him.

THE BASIS UPON WHICH THE BRETHREN ACT.—Scripture, they say, never prescribes a human commission as necessary for the church minister. Doctrine, not ordination, is the Divine test of rejecting or receiving those who profess to be ministers of Christ; and every Christian man who can do so is not only at liberty, but is bound to preach the Gospel. The parable of the talents, in Matthew xxv., teaches the danger of waiting for other warrant than the possession of the necessary gift: "And to doubt the grace of the master, or to fear because one has not the authentication of those who presumptuously claim and trifle with this right, is to bury this *talent in the* earth, and to act the part of the wicked and slothful servant." For the Lord of the harvest alone has the title to send forth labourers. In a word, say they, the question is not whether all Christians are qualified of God to preach the Gospel, but whether those who are so qualified may not preach without waiting for any human authoritative call; and Scripture, as they affirm, decides that they may. Thus, too, they argue, as to the ground of church membership. The distinction of the people and clergy they hold to be essentially a Jewish element, which afterwards crept into and undermined the church. The Christian people are the clergy. "The gifts of the Spirit are for the whole body of the church —not one of them for a particular section, but all open to the whole church, and the whole church open to all."

Rites and Ceremonies. — The doctrines held by the Brethren agree in all essentials with the Church of England and other churches of the Reformation. Their worship is conducted in the simplest manner, Circumstances apart, any brother is competent to baptize or to "break bread;" that is, administer the Lord's Supper.

They live in primitive simplicity and reject as unbecoming the luxuries of dress and furniture.

PROGRESS.—By the last census it appears that they return 141 places of worship in England and Wales; of these many are rooms in private houses; and the influence which the Brethren undoubtedly possess upon English Christianity is to be ascribed rather to their position in society, their zeal and earnestness, than their numbers. Still, their principles are adopted by a considerable body in India and the colonies, and we believe they have made some progress in America.

PRESBYTERIANS (SCOTCH).

ORIGIN.—Presbyterianism, the national religion of Scotland, known also as "THE KIRK OF SCOTLAND," was introduced by John Knox into that country, about the year 1560; Presbyterianism then having begun to assume a regular form of Church Government.

PROGRESS. — From the time of the Reformation to that of the Revolution, the Scotch Church was torn with contentions respecting her form of Church jurisdiction;* the court professing Episcopacy, and the people Presbyterianism, and each prevailed by turns; but on the accession of King William III., Presbyterianism was finally settled to be the Established Religion, and, being ratified by the Union, is still maintained in that kingdom. The Kirk now averages more than 1,000 ministers, and about 1,500,000 members. In the United States the number of Presbyterian churches is 4,591. These accommodate 2,040,506 persons. In point of numbers the orthodox Presbyterians are the third, but in wealth the first of all denominations. The total value of their church property amounts to more than 14,400,000 dollars, according to the seventh American census, published 1854.

Tenets.—Amidst the rapid revolutions in the government of the Scottish Church, the established formulary of faith seems to have remained unchanged. The Westminster Confession of Faith, which was approved and adopted by the

* Vide Article Episcopalians (Scottish).

General Assembly of the Kirk of Scotland, August 27th, 1647, and what are called the Larger and Smaller Catechisms (which are generally bound up with it), contain the public and avowed doctrines of this Church, which formularies are Calvinistical, if not Supralapsarian.

Rites and Ceremonies.—In public worship, the Creed, the Ten Commandments, and the Doxology, are not introduced; and there is no observation in this Church of those sacred Festivals referring to the events proclaiming the celestial mission of our Saviour. There is no Lent Fast; no kneeling at public prayer; no public worship of God without a sermon or public instruction; no instrumental music; no consecration of churches, or of burial-grounds; no funeral service or ceremony; no sign of the cross in baptism; no regular use of the Lord's Prayer; and no administration of the Holy Communion in private houses—not even to the sick and dying.

SCOTTISH RELIEF SYNOD.

The members of the Relief Synod are a species of Dissenters in Scotland, whose chief ground of dissent from the Establishment is, the liberty and privilege they maintain of choosing their own ministers.

ORIGIN. — The immediate occasion of this separation was the deposition from the ministry of the Rev. Mr. Gillespie, in 1752, whose professed views were different in some respects from the Presbytery. He was summoned before them, and deposed within a week.

PROGRESS.—A Rev. Mr. Boston was excluded with Mr. Gillespie; these two gentlemen, together with a Mr. Collier, of Fife, and some ordained elders, constituted themselves into a "Presbytery of Relief," and took charge of a congregation at Colinsburgh.

The Relief Synod now comprises seven presbyteries, composed of upwards of eighty congregations; and the whole number in communion with the synod is estimated at about 130,000.

Tenets.—In regard to doctrine and worship, they adhere to the standard and constitution of the Established Kirk.

Their founder, Mr. Gillespie, declared that "his views were to hold communion with all who appear to hold communion with the Head, our Lord Jesus Christ, and with such only." And their Synod has determined that it is agreeable to the principles of the Synod of Relief to hold communion with visible saints in the Episcopalian and Independent Churches.

QUAKERS (OR FRIENDS).

Origin.—This sect, which first appeared about 1648, owes its origin to an obscure individual, of the name of George Fox, a native of Drayton, in Leicestershire. Observing the vicious conduct of many professing Christians, Fox went boldly forth, preaching with great zeal against the vices they indulged in; at the same time inveighing violently against the established modes of worship, and especially against *a hired* Ministry, which he conceived to be contrary to Divine authority. This he did most indefatigably in the public market-places, at fairs, and sometimes in churches. This conduct, at length, drew upon Fox the attention of the magistrates, who, in the year 1649, committed him to prison at Nottingham; on his release, he adopted the same line of conduct as before, and suffered several subsequent imprisonments, besides enduring several persecutions.

The appellation of "*Quakers*" was bestowed upon the sect, by way of contempt; some say on account of their *tremblings* when under the impression of Divine things, which appeared in their public assemblies; but they themselves say it was first given them by one of the magistrates who committed George Fox to prison, on account of his bidding him, and those about him, *tremble* at the word of the Lord. The name of "*Quaker*," whatever was its origin, soon became their usual denomination, though they themselves adopted the appellation of "*Friends*."

PROGRESS.—Undismayed by persecution, the Friends increased rapidly, and spread themselves over the kingdom. In 1652, they first set up separate assemblies in Lancashire and the adjacent parts. In 1654, the first separate meeting of Friends was opened in London, in Watling-street. They subsequently opened a public meeting at the Bull-and-Mouth Inn, in Aldersgate-street, "where women as well as men spoke as they were moved." Bristol, Colchester, Norwich, and other large towns, were visited by their Preachers, and so great was the increase of the sect, that after the Restoration, when a fresh persecution was raised against them, George Fox, in 1662, represented to the King that 3,068 Friends had been imprisoned; while a narrative, signed by twelve witnesses, attested that "4,200 of the people called Quakers, both men and women, were in prison." The Royal Declaration of Indulgence, in 1663, suspended for a short time he furious persecution of the Quakers; but, under the Conventicle Act of 1664, numbers of Friends were condemned to transportation.

In 1666, their cause began to derive great support and credit from the distinguished abilities and virtues of the celebrated William Penn, son *of Admiral* Penn, who then joined the Society, and became one of its most eminent advocates.

In 1671, George Fox visited Barbadoes. Others occasionally had visited America at various periods, and, a number of persons having embraced the principles of the Society, George Fox came over in 1672, and settled meetings of discipline for the care of the Poor, and the Regulation of the Church. At this time there were meetings of the Friends in most of the Colonies along the seacoast, from Massachusetts as far south as the Carolinas.

In 1681, William Penn obtained from the Crown, in acquittance of a debt due to Admiral Sir William Penn, his father, a royal charter, conveying to him the tract of country denominated Pennsylvania; and in the same year he sold to a company of merchants, and others, chiefly Quakers, 20,000 acres. In 1682, William Penn arrived in the river Delaware, accompanied by 2,000 emigrants, chiefly of his own persuasion. They founded the city of Philadelphia, and settled themselves there and in the adjacent counties; in each successive year their numbers were increased by new emigrants from the mother country; and within four years, the province contained twenty settlements, and Philadelphia 2,000 inhabitants.

At the Restoration, a very severe act passed against them, the tendency of which was to compel them to take oaths; but at the Revolution their scruples were respected and relieved, and ever since 1722 their affirmation, or asseveration, has, except, we believe, in criminal cases, been considered as equivalent to an oath.

The Friends are not an increasing sect.

There are at present ten yearly meetings, viz., London, Dublin, New England, New York, Philadelphia, Baltimore, Virginia, North Carolina, Ohio, and Indiana, which include a total of about 160,000 members.

Tenets.—The Friends have no Confession of Faith independently of the Scriptures; they may, however, be considered as strict Trinitarians, and in some sense as Arminians.

The following may be looked upon as a brief sketch of their peculiar doctrines:—

I. They believe that, under the Gospel dispensation, all wars and fightings are strictly forbidden, the positive injunction of Jesus Christ entirely precluding the indulgence of those malignant passions from which such contests can arise.

II. They also apprehend that the express command of our Lord and his Apostle James, "Swear not at all," prohibits the Christian from the use of the judicial as well as other oaths.

III. With regard to the Christian Ministry, they believe that no individual has a right to assume the exclusive exercise of this Ministry in a congregation of Christians; but that all, both male and female, who are rightly moved thereto, may exercise the gift. That this Ministry being, if rightly received, received freely, and without any pecuniary expense to qualify for it, it, therefore, ought to be freely communicated, and no further support expected by Ministers than what is authorised by Christ, and was practised by his Apostles. Not feeling required to make provision for their own Ministers, whose ministry they approve, Friends deem themselves fully warranted in declining to contribute to the support of others, and of a form of worship, from both of which they conscientiously dissent.

IV. It being generally admitted that the Baptism by Water, and a participation in the Outward Supper, are but the *signs* of that essential Baptism of the Holy Ghost, instituted by Christ, and of the Communion of Saints, the Society deem these external symbols wholly unnecessary.

V. Friends consider all Holidays as "shadows," which ceased with the shadowy dispensation of the law; and that neither the first day of the week nor any other possesses any superior sanctity; seeing, moreover, that the appellation of days, months, and times are of idolatrous and superstitious original, they esteem themselves bound to follow the example of their elders, in denominating the months and days "according to the plain and Scriptural way of expression."

VI. As simplicity and gravity in dress and demeanour are consonant with the Christian character, the Society recommends its members to observe plainness in their apparel and the furniture of their houses; an adherence to the use of the singular pronouns "thee and thou," when addressing only one person; and the disuse of the customary salutations and tokens of obeisance.

RITES AND CEREMONIES.—Marriage has always been regarded by the Friends as a religious, not a mere civil, contract; all marriages are proposed at their meetings for concurrence; which is granted if upon inquiry the parties appear clear of other engagements, and if they have also the consent of their parents or guardians, without which no marriages are allowed; this Society always refused to acknowledge the exclusive authority of the priests to marry; their marriages are solemnized in a public meeting for worship; and the monthly meeting keeps a record of them, as also of the births and burials of its members.

SANDEMANIANS (OR GLASSITES).

ORIGIN.—This sect arose in Scotland about the year 1728, and were originally called Glassites, after their founder, Mr. John Glass, Minister of the parish of Tealing, near Dundee, who, having given offence to some of his brethren by avowing notions of Justifying Faith differing from those of the acknowledged Standards, was prosecuted before the Provincial Synod of Angus and Mearns, and ultimately deposed by the General Assembly in 1730.

PROGRESS.—After his deposition Mr. Glass continued to exercise his ministry; and, from among his numerous followers, he formed a congregation upon his own principles, who assembled first at Tealing, and subsequently erected a church at Dundee.

In the course of a few years, smaller congregations were "put into church order," at Edinburgh, Perth, Glasgow, and many principal towns in Scotland. Mr. Glass died in 1773, at the age of seventy-eight. In the meantime, a powerful coadjutor appeared in Mr. Robert Sandeman, an elder in one of the Scotch churches, who, having embraced Mr. Glass's principles, and grafted upon them his own peculiar views, published in 1757 "The Letters of Theron and Aspasio," which led to the well-known "Sandemanian Controversy." Chiefly, as it was commonly said, in consequence of reading those Letters, and the

Author's correspondence with Mr. S. Pike, a lecturer at Pinner's Hall, several persons in London, whither Mr. Sandeman went in 1760, became proselytes to his principles and opinions, and, in 1762, formed themselves into a congregation, which was joined, in 1765, by Mr. Pike, who became their most distinguished preacher.

Some smaller congregations were afterwards formed, upon the same principles, in different parts of England. These have been denominated Sandemanians; while in Scotland, the congregations of this communion retain the name of Glassites. Mr. Sandeman went to America in 1764, and collected several congregations in New England. He died there in 1771, at the age of fifty-three, two years before Mr. Glass. The Glassites were not at any period a numerous sect, and they are now, with the exception of a few surviving congregations, merged in other Dissenters.

TENETS.—They deem it unlawful alike to hold spiritual communion with other Churches, or to have any familiar intercourse with excommunicated persons of their own persuasion. They conceive it even unlawful to join in prayer with any one who is not a brother or a sister; and family prayer being, as they conceive, not enjoined by any express precept or precedent in the New Testament, is very generally disregarded by them.

Rites and Ceremonies.—Among their practices and observances are, the Weekly Celebration of the Lord's Supper; their Love Feasts; the Kiss of Charity on the admission of a new member, and other occasions; their abstinence from blood, and from things strangled; and washing of each others' feet.

SHAKERS (OR SHAKING QUAKERS).

Origin.—This sect, although now confined to the United States, had its rise in Lancashire.

According to a statement authorized by themselves, the Founders of the sect were James Wardley, a tailor by trade, and Jane, his wife, and the work under them began at Bolton and Manchester, about the year 1747. They had belonged to the Society of Friends; but, receiving *a further* degree of light and power, they continued for several years disconnected with every denomination. During this time they received, both by Vision and Revelation, the testimony "that the second appearance of Christ was at hand, and that the Church was rising in her full and transcendent glory."

PROGRESS.—A small Society was at length formed under their special ministry, which held its meetings alternately at Bolton and Manchester. Sometimes, after assembling together, and sitting awhile in silent meditation, they were taken with a mighty trembling, under which they would express the indignation of God against all sin. At other times they were affected, under the power of God, with a mighty *shaking!* and they were occasionally exercised in singing, shouting, or walking the floor under the influence of spiritual signs, swiftly passing and re-passing each other. From these strange exercises, the people received the name of "Shakers," which, though intended in derision, they acknowledge to be properly applied to them.

The work went on, under Wardley, till the year 1770, when a new impulse was given to the

Society by Ann Lee. She was the daughter of blacksmith of Manchester; where she also, at an early age, became the wife of a blacksmith. She was herself a cutter of hatters' fur. She had joined the Society about 1758, and was now recognised as the Leader of the Sect. She was addressed as "the Elect Lady," and "the Mother Elect," "the first Spiritual Parent in the line of the Covenant," &c. To such as addressed her by her proper name, she would reply, "I am Ann the Word!"

These impious arrogations having been made the subject of a criminal prosecution, she was committed to prison, and afterwards confined in a madhouse. To escape from further persecution, in 1774 she set sail for New York with her husband, brother, and other followers, and in that State this strange sect has found the means of perpetuating itself. Her first community was formed at Watervliet, near Albany, where she died in 1784.

Dr. Dwight states, "that she claimed the *power* to work Miracles, and to speak with *Tongues.*" Societies were soon organised at

Lebanon, in New York, and at Enfield, in Connecticut, and have gradually increased to their present number, which averages 5,000. Their property is all in common; and the members are distinguished for their industry and morality. Celibacy is enjoined; and the sect is kept up entirely by proselytes. The office of Leader is bestowed by impulse or revelation on him who has the gift to assume it. Dr. Dwight says, "The power of working Miracles they still claim. They declare that they have visions of the invisible world, and that spirits converse with them."

SOUTHCOTTONIANS.

Origin.—This sect of singular fanatics took their rise from Johannah Southcott, a vulgar visionary, whose extraordinary pretensions attracted a numerous band of converts in London and its vicinity. She was born in the West of England, about the year 1750, of parents in a very humble sphere of life, and while in service at Exeter, being carried away either by a heated imagination, or determined imposture, it being extremely difficult to decide which, gave herself out as the Woman spoken of in Revelations, persuading herself that she held converse with the Devil, and communion with the Holy Ghost; and, although warned of her delusion by a Dissenting minister, she found some clergymen of the Establishment credulous enough to countenance her pretensions.

Progress.—In 1792 she assumed the character of a Prophetess, and of the "Woman in the Wilderness;" and began to give sealed papers to her followers, which were called her "Seals," and which were to protect both from the judgments of the present and a future life. They are said to have been applied for by thousands.

Although in the highest degree illiterate, she turned author, and wrote a mass of unintelligible nonsense, delivering her predictions both in prose and doggrel rhyme. These effusions, besides containing some personal threatenings against her opponents, related principally to impending judgments upon the surrounding nations, and the speedy approach of the Millennium.

In 1814, after she had passed her grand climacteric, she was seized with a disorder which subsequently gave her the outward appearance of pregnancy, and she announced herself as the mother of the Shiloh, promised by Jacob, whose speedy advent she predicted. Some months before this period she had given notice of her supposed situation, and invited the opinion of the faculty. Several of them admitted her pregnancy (among whom was Dr. Reece); others doubted; and some (among whom was Dr. Sims) absolutely denied it. Her followers, however, were full of confidence, and some of them, who were rich, made many costly presents, particularly a Bible, which cost forty pounds; and a superb cot (or cradle) made of the most expensive materials, and highly decorated, the value of which was two hundred pounds. About ten weeks before Christmas she was confined to her bed, and took very little sustenance, until at last pain and sickness reduced her to the lowest state of human existence. Mr. Want, a surgeon, warned her of her approaching end, and prescribed some medicine to alleviate her sufferings, but she was deaf to advice, and insisted that all her sufferings were only preparatory to the birth of the Shiloh. Subsequently, however, she had some misgivings, during some comparatively lucid intervals, in which she declared that "if she was deceived, she had, at all events, been the sport of some spirit, either good or evil." She also, at the last, admitted the possibility of a temporary dissolution; and expressly ordered that means should be taken to preserve warmth in her for four days, after which she was to revive and be delivered; or, in failure, she gave permission to be opened.

December 27th, she actually died, and the symptoms were so decisive, that her disciples had no hope but in her Resurrection. At the end, however, of four days and nights, the body appeared discoloured, and exhibited signs of approaching putrefaction. She was then opened in the presence of fifteen medical men, when it was ascertained that her complaints arose from bile and flatulency, from indulgence and want of exercise. Her remains were conveyed for interment, *under* a fictitious name, to the burying-ground attached to the chapel in St. John's Wood, where a large tombstone, containing quotations from the Bible, and her own writings, has been erected by her determined followers, who still remain unconvinced of their delusion—not being undeceived, either by her death or dissection.

SWEDENBORGIANS.

Origin.—This sect derive their origin and their name from Baron Swedenborg, a learned Swede, born at Stockholm in 1688, and who died in London in 1772.

In 1743, the Baron asserts, "The Lord manifested himself to him in a personal appearance, and at the same time opened his spiritual eyes, so that he was enabled constantly to see and converse with saints and angels." He shortly afterwards began to print and publish the revelations obtained by intercourse with the World of Spirits. These mystical works, all of which bear extraordinary titles, commenced in 1749, and terminated in 1771. They consist of fourteen quarto volumes, and numerous small treatises.

Progress.—After Baron Swedenborg's decease, his theological writings began to attract much more notice than they had obtained in his lifetime They were much sought after, and speedily translated from the Latin into German, English, and French. His works now found numerous readers, and no fewer than fifty clergymen of the Established Church of England are stated, at this time, to have become satisfied of the truth of Swedenborg's revelations. About 1788, a number of his disciples formed themselves into a distinct religious society, under the name of "The New Jerusalem Church;" and at a General Conference of the members, held in London in 1788, a summary of the doctrines of the New Church, extracted from the Baron's writings by a committee of his followers, was adopted as the authentic exposition of their creed; and a general Liturgy has since been drawn up.

A General Conference is now held annually. At the Fifteenth Conference, held in Manchester, in August, 1822, there were eight ministers and thirty-seven delegates, representing twenty-four congregations. The number of recognised members in Great Britain was at that time estimated at between 2,500 and 3,000; but the number of attendants and general favourers of the doctrines was far greater. In Lancashire, where they are most numerous, they were supposed to amount to 10,000. In London they have now three chapels. In Scotland they have three or four small congregations. In Ireland three, but in Wales none.

In the United States of America the Swedenborgians average about 4,600. In Sweden there are a few who have embraced these tenets, but they are not allowed the public exercise of their worship; and other believers in Swedenborg are scattered over the Continent.

TENETS.—The leading doctrine of this Church, as inculcated in the writings of the Baron, relates to the person of Jesus Christ, and to the redemption wrought, not purchased by Him. On this subject it is insisted that Jesus Christ is Jehovah, manifested in the flesh, and that he came into the world to glorify his human nature, by making it one with the Divine. It is, therefore, insisted further, that the humanity of Jesus

Christ is itself Divine, by virtue of its indissoluble union with the indwelling Father, and that thus, as to his humanity, He is the Mediator between God and man, since there is no other medium of God's access to man, or of man's access to God, but this Divine humanity, which was assumed for this purpose. Thus it is taught, that in the person of Jesus Christ dwells the whole Trinity of Father, Son, and Holy Spirit.

On the subject of the Redemption wrought by this Incarnate God, it is taught, that it consisted, not in the vicarious sacrifice of one God, so as to satisfy the justice or to appease the wrath of another God, but in the real subjugation of the Powers of Darkness and their removal from man, by continual combats and victories over them, during His abode in the world; and in the consequent descent to man of divine power and life, which was brought near to him in the thus glorified humanity of this combating God.

Rites and Ceremonies. — The Swedenborgians retain the two Sacraments of Baptism and the Lord's Supper, which they say are the only *rites insisted* on by the author.

SYRIAN CHRISTIANS.

The Origin of this Indian branch of the Syrian Church, which still exists in Travancore and Cochin, is involved in obscurity.

The Syrian Christians formerly enjoyed political ascendancy in Malabar. When Vasco de Gama reached India in 1503, he was shewn the sceptre of the last Christian King of Malayala. The Portuguese Missionaries were surprised to find upwards of a hundred Christian Churches on the coast of Malabar. When they acquired sufficient power, they compelled the native Christians on the seacoast to acknowledge the supremacy of the Pope; but the Churches of the interior refused to yield to Rome, and, under the protection of the native princes, maintained their ecclesiastical independence.

It is stated that these Christians are still divided into those who adhere to their primitive Tenets, called "Syrian Christians of Malayala;" and those who have adopted the Ordinances of the Papal See, and who are called "Syro-Roman Catholics." Of the former class there are fifty-seven churches or congregations, comprehending about 16,500 families, or 74,000 individuals; of the latter there are a hundred-and-seven churches, the congregations belonging to which amount to 100,000 persons; besides which, there is a large number of converts obtained from other tribes, making a total of 180,000 persons.

TENETS.—The creed of the "Syrian Christians" is assimilated to that of the Western Churches; the Liturgy is that which was formerly used in the Churches of the Patriarchate of Antioch, which Patriarch they acknowledge as their head.

RITES AND CEREMONIES. — These resemble those of the Greek Church. No sculptured images are admitted except crucifixes; but paintings are seen in all the churches, in which the Virgin is always the chief personage. Much incense is also used.

UNITARIANS.

ORIGIN. — Unitarianism in England dates almost as far back as the earliest translation of *the Bible*; for Strype, in his Memoirs of Archbishop Cranmer, says: — "There were now (1548) other heresies vented abroad, as the denial of the Trinity and the Deity of the Holy Ghost." In 1551, a German named George Van Paris was burned at London for this heresy; and four years after, another person at Uxbridge. Joan Bocher, sometimes called "The Maid of Kent," was a more distinguished victim. She was a lady of family and education, and possessed heroic courage. Edward VI. could hardly be prevailed upon to consent to her execution; and signed the warrant, saying to Cranmer that he must be responsible for the sin.

PROGRESS.—Notwithstanding persecution, the sect increased, so much so, that under James I. a large number of persons, some of them of rank and consideration, were executed for the same offence. During the Commonwealth they seem to have met with milder treatment. John Biddle, their leader, was at last, however, thrown by Cromwell into prison, where he died in 1662. An act of the Long Parliament, making the profession of Unitarianism a felony, was mitigated by William III., and repealed altogether in 1813; and they now stand on the same footing as all other Dissenters from the Established Church.

Dr. Priestley may be considered as the founder of the modern Unitarian School in this country; to his writings and influence the progress of Unitarian principles, during the latter part of the last century, may be chiefly ascribed; among his coadjutors may be mentioned the Rev. Theophilus Lindsey, a beneficed clergyman, who, in 1773, resigned his living, and afterwards preached to a congregation of his own principles in Essex-street, Strand, London. The attendance was at no time numerous; nor can it be said the sect has greatly increased, although they received a powerful aid from the abilities and ministry of Mr. Belsham.

The number of congregations in England is about two hundred and fifty. In Scotland and Ireland there are, besides these, about fifty congregations.

Their Colleges at Hackney, Exeter, and Warrington are all extinct; and that at York, which alone survives, is sustained by orthodox endowments.

In France, many of the Protestant Clergy reject the Trinitarian scheme of Christian doctrine; the principal sources of supply for the French ministry of the French Churches are the schools of Geneva and Montauban, where the Unitarian system has the ascendancy. In 1832 a society was formed in Paris, called the Unitarian Association of France.

In British Asia a native society of Unitarian Christians has existed for several years at Madras, under the care of William Roberts, a native; but a much more remarkable development of opinion of this kind occurred in the case of the distinguished Brahmin, the late Rammohun Roy, of Calcutta, who in his publications in English, called "The Precepts of Jesus," and also in his "First," "Second," and "Final Appeal to the Christian Public," has directed and influenced the thoughts of numbers of his countrymen to the Anti-Trinitarian doctrines therein promulgated, and was, since 1827, to the period of his decease, associated with distinguished individuals, of both the native and European population, in the support of Christian worship according to the Unitarian faith.

In America, Unitarian opinions appear to have been extensively adopted in Massachusetts, as early as the last century. In 1756 appeared "Emlyn's Humble Inquiry into the Scripture Account of Jesus Christ;" this work was published at Boston, and had an extensive circulation. In 1785 one of the three Episcopal Churches of that city adopted a Liturgy, excluding the recognition of the Trinitarian doctrine. In 1786 Mr. Lindsey had opened a correspondence with the Anti-Trinitarians in America, and, having received intelligence of the spread of Unitarianism, induced Dr. Priestley's emigration thither in 1794: he formed a congregation at Philadelphia. In 1819 a congregation was gathered at Baltimore, and others now exist in New York, Philadelphia, Washington, Charleston, Pittsburg, Cincinnati, and other principal cities of the Union.

In America, the Unitarians are divided into two classes: "The Congregational," and "The

Christian." The number of churches organized according to the Congregational form average from 180 to 200; while the denomination called Christians, which is numerous, particularly in the Western States, reckon from 900 to 1,000 churches.

TENETS.—Unitarians profess to derive their views from Scripture, and to make it the ultimate arbiter in all religious questions. They undertake to show that, interpreted according to the settled laws of language, the uniform testimony of the Sacred Writings is, that the Holy Spirit has no personal existence, distinct from the Father; and that the Son is a derived and dependent Being, whether, as some believe, created in some remote period of time, or, as others, beginning to live when He appeared on earth.

They insist that ecclesiastical history enables them to trace to obsolete systems of heathen philosophy the introduction of the received doctrine into the Church, in which, once received, it has been sustained on grounds quite independent of its merits; and they aver that it is satisfactorily refuted by the Biblical passages, when rightly understood, which are customarily adduced in its support.

UNIVERSALISTS.

The great doctrine of Universalism is that the sufferings of the wicked after death are purgatorial in their character, and will finally be terminated in eternal happiness. This doctrine is fundamental; but it is held, of course, in conjunction with many others.

Universalists may, however, now be divided into two parties, the Evangelical or Orthodox, and those who embrace Arian or Unitarian sentiments. Of the latter it is unnecessary to give any detailed account, since, in fact, they form a part, by far the larger part, of the Unitarian body. The process by which Universalism has linked itself with Sociniasm has been the result of a mutual attraction. Great numbers of those who began with Unitarianism have advanced in the course of their speculations to Universalism; and, on the other hand, not a few of those who set out for Universalism have cast aside the orthodox creed to embrace the doctrines of Socinus.

Universalism professes to rest in part upon critical exegesis, but more fully perhaps upon philosophical argument. Under the former, those texts of Scripture are argued and explained in which our Lord and the sacred writers have been generally supposed to assert the eternity of future punishment. Under the latter, the benevolence of the Deity, the proper ends of punishment, and similar considerations, are advanced. Nor does Universalism hesitate to make its appeals to the Christian Fathers, and to claim their sanction. But few traces of the doctrine, it is admitted, are to be found in the first and second centuries. During this period no controversies had arisen on the subject. Clemens, of Alexandria, is claimed as one of the Fathers, who, during this period, held these doctrines. Daille and Archbishop Potter admit the justice of the charge, the truth of which, from the diffuseness of the Father's writings, it is no easy matter to determine. "It is manifest," says the former, "throughout his work, that

Clemens thought all the punishments that God inflicts upon men are salutary, and executed by him only for the purpose of instruction and reformation. Of this kind he reckons the torments which the damned in hell suffer."

Origen was the pupil of Clemens, and may be considered as the founder of Universalism in the early Church. About the year 230 he published his book, "De Principiis," in which he advocates at length the doctrine of universal salvation. It forms part of a system which exposed him to the charge of heresy in his own time, and has ranked him ever since amongst the fanciful and visionary. In connection with Universalism he held the doctrine of pre-existence. His opinion was, that in the past ages of eternity God created, at once, all the rational minds which have ever existed, whether of angels or men, gave them the same nature and the same powers, and placed them all in one celestial state. Accordingly they were all, at first, exactly alike in rank, capacity, and character. But as they all had perfect freedom of will, they did not long continue in this state of equality; for, while some improved themselves more or less, others degenerated proportionally, till an infinite diversity of character and condition began to take place among them. In consequence of this the Almighty at length formed the material universe out of pre-existent matter, and appointed those spirits to different ranks and conditions in it according to their respective deserts; elevating some to the angelic order, consigning others to the infernal abodes as demons, and sending the intermediate class, as occasion might require, into human bodies. All these intelligent beings still retain their original freedom of will, and are, therefore, capable of returning from their former transgressions, or of rising to still higher degrees of excellence. The fall of man, in his view, consisted in the descent of the celestial soul to the prison of an earthly body, in consequence of its transgressions in a pre-existent state. In the resurrection mankind will come forth with bodies not of gross earthy matter, but of an aërial substance; and then the whole human race, both good and bad, will be subjected to a fiery ordeal in the general conflagration, with different degrees of pain, according to their moral purity or corruption. The righteous will quickly pass through this trial into the enjoyment of heaven; but the wicked will then be condemned to the punishments of hell, which consist both of inflicted pain and of the remorse of conscience. These sufferings, though he calls them everlasting, Origen held, would be apportioned in length and severity to each one's wickedness and hardness of heart; but for others, especially for the devil, they would necessarily be rendered intense, and protracted to an immense duration, in order to overcome the obstinacy and corruption of the guilty sufferers. At last, however, the whole intelligent creation should be purified, and God become all in all. His opinions lingered in the Church, and even gained ground.

Modern Universalists claim St. Basil, Bishop of Cæsarea, his brother the Bishop of Nyssa, Gregory Nazianzen, in the fourth century, as more or less inclined to the sentiments of Origen on the nature of future punishments.

Universalism appears to have been for a time

the opinion of a majority of the Fathers in the Eastern Church. Gregory Dysson, Didymus, and Jerome, were, to some extent, its advocates. The father of the modern Universalists was James Relly, originally a friend and follower of George Whitfield. Relly began his ministerial career in Mr. Whitfield's, or Lady Huntingdon's connexion; but, gradually renouncing the doctrines he had once espoused, he taught that Christ, as a mediator, was united to mankind, and, by his obedience and sufferings, had as fully restored the whole human race to the divine favour as if all had obeyed or suffered in their own persons. Rellian Universalism, as it has been called, has the system of Calvin for its basis. His creed is thus stated by one of his followers, Mr. Whittemore, in his "Modern History of Universalism:"—"Jesus Christ had made satisfaction for all the human race, and bore their sins in his body: hence he knows nothing of inflicting the demands of justice upon the sinner. Sin is to be dreaded for the natural evils which it brings in its train, but not for the penalty of the divine law, which we have all suffered to the full in the person of Jesus. Thus, although Relly admitted the doctrine of partial suffering in the future state, he maintained that the state of unbelievers, after death, cannot be a state of punishment, because Jesus Christ, who hath tasted death for every man, bore the chastisements of their peace when the Lord laid upon him the iniquities of us all. He admitted the doctrine of misery in the future state only on the principle that while in unbelief men know not, nor believe, that Jesus hath put away their sins by the sacrifice of himself; and, therefore, they are oppressed with guilt and fear; and these are in proportion to their use or abuse of knowledge—to their receiving, or obstinately rejecting the divine evidences and demonstrations of grace and salvation. But he looked beyond all evil and misery, whether in this or the future state, to a time of universal restitution, when all mankind will be brought to know the Lamb of God, who hath taken away the sins of the world."

There are at present only two principal societies in Great Britain, known as Universalists, *which* maintain, in other respects, orthodox sentiments, "all holding, and all rejoicing to hold, as essential tenets of Christianity, the supreme deity of Jesus Christ, the efficacy of his atoning sacrifice, the power of his resurrection, new creation of his Spirit through his Word, the election of his Church, and the inheritance of his kingdom by the members of that Church alone." These are, first, a body at Glasgow, among whom are some of the friends and followers of Mr. Neil Douglas, who is regarded as the father of Universalism in Sotland; and a second, a Church at Plymouth.

The congregation in Liverpool, under the pastoral care of the Rev. Dr. David Thom, who presided over it for a period of more than thirty years, after his death, in 1862, became entirely dispersed, some attending one place of worship, some another.

The principles once maintained by the Liverpool Society are thus briefly stated by the late Dr. Thom:—"We love the leading doctrines of the Gospel, not as they appear in popular creeds, but as they are laid down in the Scriptures themselves. We know no teacher of divine truth but the Holy Ghost himself, speaking to us and teaching us in and through Holy Scriptures. Nevertheless we can love and admire the statements of divine truth which are to be found in the Thirty-nine Articles of the Church of England, and in other publications, the leading views of which rest upon evangelical principles. To us Universalism is a truth, because God himself reveals it; but it is not to us the main truth. Hence we very seldom speak of it. Regeneration by the Spirit of Christ Jesus, admission into the enjoyment of his knowledge and love, and the fruits and effects which spring from the influence and operation of the truth, are our constant, as they are scriptural themes."

Universalism in America had diffused itself to an extent, and had come to possess amongst its supporters an amount of talent, energy, and influence, calculated to give it a high standing amongst the religious denominations of the great transatlantic republic. About the year 1840, after many bickerings, and the exhibition of much unpleasant feeling, they split into two subordinate divisions denominated the Impartialists and the Restorationists. The former, who are by far the more numerous of the two bodies, deny the existence of an intermediate state of happiness and misery, the infliction of temporary torments, and the natural immorality of the soul; maintaining, that although there is a distinction between believers and unbelievers in time, this distinction, nevertheless, extends no further; the whole human family, after having died, continuing till the end of time in a state of unconsciousness, and the rising again all at once, and without any distinctiou, to the enjoyment of eternal life. The latter maintain the immortality of the soul, the existence of an intermediate state, torments inflicted upon the wicked during a longer or shorter period, the reign of the saints, and the ultimate restoration through them of all things by Christ. These, it will be seen, are the sentiments of the older Universalists.

JUDAISM.

JUDAISM means the religious doctrines and rites of the Jews, who are the descendants of Abraham. A complete system of Judaism is contained in the five books of Moses.

The Talmud is a collection of the doctrines and morality of the Jews. They have two works that bear this name: the first is called the Talmud of Jerusalem, and the other the Talmud of Babylon. The former is more obscure, and the Jews prefer the one compiled at Babylon, which is clearer and more extensive.

The principal sects among the Jews, in the time of our Saviour, were the Pharisees, who placed religion in external ceremony; the Sadducees, who were remarkable for their incredulity; and the Essenes, distinguished by an austere severity.

At present the Jews have two sects, the Caraites, who admit no rule of religion but the law of Moses; and the Rabbinists, who add to the laws the tradition of the Talmud.

The expectation of a Messiah is the distinguishing feature of their religious system. The word Messiah signifies one anointed, or installed into office by unction. The Jews, infatuated with the idea of a temporal Messiah, who is to subdue the world, still wait for his appearance.

The most remarkable periods in the history of the Jews are, the call of Abraham, the giving of the law by Moses, their establishment in Canaan under Joshua, the building of the Temple of Solomon, their Captivity in Babylon, their return under Zerubbabel, and the destruction of their city and temple by Titus.

It is impossible to fix the number of persons this nation is at present composed of. But yet we have reason to believe that there are nearly three millions who profess this religion, and, as their phrase is, are witness of the unity of God, in all nations of the world.

MAHOMETANISM.

MAHOMETANISM is the religion of Mahomet, who was born in 571, at Mecca, a city of Arabia, and died at Medina, in 631. Mahomet, though descended from an honourable tribe and the noblest family, yet his original lot was poverty; through marriage, however, he became equal to the most opulent in Mecca. Fifteen years of his life he passed in the obscurest retirement, in a lonely cave, where his scheme of a new religion was no doubt planned.

Mahometanism is a compound of Paganism, Judaism, and Christianity; the Koran, which is the Bible of the Mahometans, is held in great reverence. The great doctrine of the Koran is the Unity of God, which, together with the mission of Christ, is strongly insisted upon by the prophet. It was communicated, says Mahomet, by the ministration of the angel Gabriel, his angel of death, whose province it is, at the hour of dissolution, to free the departing spirit from its *prison* of flesh; and his vast ideal balance, in *which* at the last day the actions of all men shall be weighed, have in them a sort of romantic sublimity, calculated to impress the fervid imagination of the eastern nations. His sensual paradise hereafter, must, in their opinion, have imparted to it the highest degree of perfection: "The meauest in paradise shall have a tent assigned to him of pearls, hyacinths, and emeralds."

When we peruse the Koran, and examine the materials of which it is composed—when we observe how much the work is indebted to the Jewish and Christian Revelations—when we see with how mnch art the whole is accommodated to the opinions and habits of the Jews, Christians, and Pagans—when we consider what indulgences it grants, and what future scenes it unfolds; and, more than all, when we contemplate the Reformer at the head of a conquering army, the Koran in one hand, and in the other a sword, we cannot be surprised at the civil and religious revolution which has immortalised his name.

Mahometanism distributes itself into two general parts, Faith and Practice—the former containing six branches—Belief in God, in his angels, in his scriptures, in his prophets, and in the resurrection and final judgment in the divine decrees; the latter relating to prayer, with washing, alms, fasting, pilgrimage to Mecca, and circumcision.

The Mahometan religion is established in, or prevails throughout the Turkish dominions, in Europe, Asia, and Africa, namely, Romania, Bulgaria, Greece, Candia, Cyprus, Natolia, Syria, part of Armenia, Egypt, &c.; the Barbary States, namely, Morocco, Algiers, Tunis, Tripoli, Fez, &c. It has likewise made many proselytes in various other countries, as in China, &c. The number of those professing the Mahometan religion has been calculated to amount to about 142 millions.

THE RELIGIONS OF THE GLOBE.

As we have given the number of each sect, it will perhaps be interesting to the reader to know the number of the inhabitants of the globe professing the different religions.

If we suppose, according to the usual estimates, that the inhabitants of the globe amount to 897,000,000, then the whole may be thus divided :—

Jews	3,000,000
Pagans	482,000,000
Christians	270,000,000
Mahometans	142,000,000

The Christians again may thus be distributed:—

Greek and Eastern Churches .	60,000,000
Protestants	80,000,000
Roman Catholics . . .	130,000,000

CPSIA information can be obtained
at www.ICGtesting.com
Printed in the USA
LVHW111638170422
716440LV00006B/633

9 783752 594003